The

INVESTIGATIONS

of

SHERLOCK HOLMES

Reminiscences of John Watson, M.D.

Edited by John Heywood

Paperback ISBN 9781780926070
ePub ISBN 9781780926087
PDF ISBN 9781780926094

Published in the UK by MX Publishing
335 Princess Park Manor, Royal Drive, London,
N11 3GX. United Kingdon
www.mxpublishing.com

Cover by www.staunch.com

CONTENTS

The Ships Chandler of Hyde

IT IS NO SURPRISE that many of the mysteries and crimes which my friend Mr Sherlock Holmes has made the subject of his life's work should have arisen in some of the most dangerous and sinister corners of this land. Crime is a disease, and that it should flourish in healthy surroundings is hardly to be expected. Yet it must be acknowledged that the opium-dens of Limehouse and the mires of Dartmoor hold no monopoly on horror. On the contrary, it has often been the most salubrious of places that have produced the most grotesque of crimes. It was in the ancient and respectable mansions of the Reigate squires, readers may remember, that an outbreak of blackmail and murder erupted, as it was in the idyllic countryside of Lamberly that the dark secret of the Sussex Vampire lay hidden. Perhaps, indeed, no setting is so innocent that it is safe from the intrusion of crime, no Eden so perfect that it may not conceal its serpent. What more harmless a place could one find than the beach of a seaside holiday town? and yet even there danger may lurk, unsuspected by the innocent holiday-maker. One such instance Holmes himself chronicled under the title of 'The Lion's Mane', and reading that narrative brought to my mind another seaside mystery, one of many years ago. It involved a ships chandler by the name of Meredith, who was found washed up on a Norfolk beach. I have hitherto been reluctant to lay the facts of the case before the public, but Mr Meredith's recent death has freed me to do so. Although it remained a private matter, which never came to the attention of the police or the public, I nonetheless offer this brief account of the affair, as it affords a glimpse of Sherlock Holmes at a time when, though his fame was in its infancy, his formidable powers were already at their height.

It was August in London, and the dog days of summer were upon us. All London seemed deserted. The Courts of Justice and the Houses of Parliament were in recess; the drawing-rooms of fashionable Mayfair were draped and silent, abandoned by their noble owners for the fresher air of Monte Carlo or Baden-Baden; the little offices and shops in every suburb from Kennington to Kentish Town were closed, the clerks and shopkeepers having locked the shutters and taken their families to the sea-side; and only the poorest, it seemed, remained in London, obliged to bear the heat until September, when at last they would be able to flee the metropolis for the hop-fields of Kent.

My friend Sherlock Holmes spent much of his time during this period upon the sofa, restlessly turning from book to newspaper and back again, or merely lying supine, eyeing through half-closed lids the morphine bottle on the mantelpiece. It was not so much the heat that affected him, for his lean and wiry frame was able to withstand the hottest weather, as the prolonged inaction imposed on him by a city in siesta. His mind fretted for lack of any useful activity, and every day of enforced idleness that passed sapped his spirit further. Our Baker street flat was littered with the apparatus of abandoned chemical experiments and other unsuccessful attempts to cheat the *ennui* that lay in wait for him. As one empty week succeeded another, he grew ever more listless and restive, pacing the drawing-room of our flat in his dressing-gown or lying on the sofa which had become his day-bed, bemoaning the lack of crime.

On one such morning I came down to breakfast to find Holmes in his dressing-gown, reading the morning paper. So haphazard were his hours at this period that I had not the least idea whether he had risen early or not yet gone to bed. Mrs Hudson had prepared us a light breakfast, but he was absorbed in the paper and did not trouble to come to the table; as I sat down to eat, he remained on the sofa, alternately re-reading the paper and staring into space.

"Anything interesting in the newspaper?" I asked him as I poured myself another cup of coffee. "You don't tell me the criminal world is finally stirring itself?"

He flung the paper over to me. "Perhaps it is, Watson, perhaps it is. The report is on page three. What do you make of it?"

I began to read.

" 'SHOCKING THEFT
Priceless Artefacts Stolen from Eade Castle.

Staff at Eade Castle this morning found the castle's famous drawing-room denuded of all its most valuable treasures. A painting by Giorgione, an unique Louis Quinze roll-top escritoire, and the whole of Lord Eade's unparalleled collection of -' "

"No, no, Watson! No more, I beg you," Holmes interrupted me, raising his long, bony hand in a gesture of pained refusal. "A catalogue of his Lordship's collection is more than I could stand in this heat. That is not the report that interests me. Try further down the page."

I tried again.

" 'Whitsea. ANOTHER VICTIM OF THE BLORE SANDS. We regret to report a most unfortunate, but not unfamiliar, accident yesterday in the popular sea-side resort of Whitsea. Our correspondent sends the following account:

Mr Samuel Meredith, the ships chandler of Hyde, ran into difficulties while bathing in the sea at Blore Bay, where the tidal currents are notoriously strong and unpredictable. His struggles were seen by Mr Brown, a passing holiday-maker, who, being a strong swimmer, entered the waves to attempt a rescue. Unhappily, the tide proved the stronger, forcing the intrepid visitor back to the shore alone. Mr Meredith was swept away, and it is to be feared that he has become the latest victim of these notoriously dangerous waters.' "

"Well, what do you make of that?" he asked.

"What a sad business! One moment a fellow is enjoying his summer's holiday at the sea-side, and the next, he is swept away to his death. I wonder if he had a wife and children? It's a terrible thing, Holmes, I agree, a terrible thing. All the same, I'm at a loss to see any suggestion of crime in this unhappy accident."

"One or two curious details in the report suggest otherwise to me."

4

"Really? What details are they?"

"Well, take Meredith's address, for instance. He was the keeper of the ships chandlery at Hyde, we are told. Do you know where Hyde is?"

"I can't say that I do."

"Let us suppose it to be a little place a few miles along the coast from Whitsea, and –"

" 'Suppose'?" I interjected with some impatience. "Come, Holmes, either you know the place or you don't. This is mere random conjecture."

"Not at all, my dear fellow. A reasoned hypothesis is not mere conjecture. I see you doubt me; let us take the points one by one. You and I enjoy between us a pretty good knowledge of England; had it been a town of any size, we would know of it. Hence, a little place. As for its being on the coast, where would you expect to find a ships chandlery? In the cabbage-fields of Bedfordshire? In surmising it close to Whitsea, I am on shakier ground, I admit, but still, it is the most likely reading. Remember, the newspaper report was sent in from Whitsea. Why, if the Whitsea correspondent bothers to mention Hyde at all, does he not tell his readers where it is? Why did he not write 'a ships-chandler from Hyde, in Dorset', let us say? That would be the usual style. I suggest that he doesn't tell his readers where Hyde is because they already know; in other words, it is a local place. Well, I wonder if my conclusions are right," said he, reaching behind him for the gazetteer. "Let me see . . . Norfolk . . . here we are. 'Hyde; village lying on the German Ocean, 6 miles east-south-east of Whitsea. Population 430, &c., &c.' Now, the inhabitants . . . ah! Here is our man: 'Meredith, Samuel, ships-chandler'. So, Watson, this man Meredith was a local tradesman. Now, does that suggest anything to you?"

"I can't say that it does."

"No? To me it suggests that this drowning was not an accident."

I was somewhat bewildered by this interpretation, which seemed to me quite fanciful. I could not but wonder if my friend's usually acute judgement had been blunted by weeks of inaction.

"Why does his being a local man make any difference to the case?" I asked. "For the matter of that, why be surprised at another drowning? What is suspicious about it? After all, these sands, the Blore Sands, have drowned a number of unfortunates in the past. They are well known to be utterly treacherous, if the newspaper writer is to be believed."

"Precisely, my dear Watson, precisely!" he answered, stabbing the air with his forefinger. "The sands, as you say, are notorious. A holiday-maker who knew nothing of their evil repute might have bathed there and drowned – indeed, many have done just that – but a local man must surely know of the danger. Why would he swim there?"

"It's beyond me, Holmes. Perhaps the fellow was drunk."

"Ha! Watson, you think that idleness has led me to imagine crimes where none exist, do you not? No, no, don't trouble to deny it; in your eyes I am like the parched traveller in the desert who sees before him a lake of clear water, when he is in truth surrounded by nothing but sand." He sighed wearily and relapsed onto the sofa. "Well, perhaps you are right. Perhaps what we have here is just another drowning, some sad mishap of no evil import whatever. I suppose we shall never know. If there was indeed foul play, the culprit will have already fled.

And whatever the circumstances, it seems the chandler is dead, and beyond any man's help."

"So it seems," I replied, and continued reading the paper. I found little to interest me until I came to the back page.

"Listen to this, Holmes, in the Stop Press! *'WHITSEA DROWNING. Man found alive on Hyde beach early this morning, believed Saml. Meredith, chandler, formerly feared drowned.'*"

"Well done, Watson! A triumph for your thorough and methodical reading habits. I had missed it. This is a most interesting development. It seems the chandler is not, after all, beyond help. Indeed, unless I am much mistaken, he is sorely in need of it. I am inclined to look into this matter. Perhaps you would have the goodness to look up the trains in Bradshaw. I propose to show you, friend Watson, that I am still *compos mentis*, and that this crime is not the mere figment of a mind made delirious by heat and idleness. What say you to a trip to the sea-side?"

So it was that Sherlock Holmes and I found ourselves, later that morning, on the train to Whitsea. Although we had the compartment to ourselves, Holmes was not a convivial travelling-companion. Most of the journey he spent in silence, smoking his pipe and gazing out at the passing fields. Only after he had produced a veritable pea-souper of tobacco-smoke in our compartment did he take the pipe from his mouth. He pointed at me with its stem: "We must proceed with care, Watson; if my suspicions are justified, and there has been foul play, then there is danger that more foul play will follow. I trust that you remembered to bring your service revolver?"

"I did."

"Excellent! Let us hope it will not be needed. On our arrival, I shall remain in Whitsea and gather what information I may about the matter."

"And I?"

"You are to go at once to Hyde, if you will, to Mr Meredith's establishment, the chandlery. Find out all you can about the man. Talk to his wife, to his servant, to his serving-assistant. Leave no stone unturned, Watson. The slightest hint, the most trivial piece of information may turn out to be of the utmost importance."

"I understand."

"When you have finished at Hyde, return to Whitsea. We shall compare our findings and we see where they have led us. And we do not have long to wait," said he, looking out of the window. "This is Whitsea now."

At Whitsea station there was a carriage-stand, but no carriage. A boy informed us that his 'guv'nor' would be back within the half-hour. Holmes suggested that in the meantime we might be able to furnish ourselves with some more information about the disappearance of Meredith. I supposed we might apply to the police-station for this information, or perhaps to the office of the local newspaper, but my companion thought otherwise.

"We need not look so far afield, Watson." He nodded towards a large public-house that stood before us. "Here is the most likely source of the information we seek. We had better enter separately. Do you go in here, and wait. I shall join you shortly." And so saying he left me at the door of the saloon, and went on to the public bar.

When he wishes to use it, Sherlock Holmes commands an insinuating charm which enables him to extract information without his companion ever having the least awareness of being so used. I took my seat in the saloon and, a glass of cool beer on the table before me, looked across into the public bar, where I could see Holmes chatting and drinking with four or five local men. After some twenty minutes he joined me.

"Well, Watson, there have been developments since the matter was reported in this morning's newspapers. Meredith was indeed washed up alive, in the dark hours of yesterday morning, near Hyde. He was taken to the church hall of St Olaf's, where the churchwardens installed him in a small private room. A doctor was in attendance, and one of the churchwardens and his wife undertook to invigilate. Throughout the day he lay close to death, vacillating between unconsciousness and delirium, and yesterday evening he received the last sacraments. All last night his life lay in the balance, but by dawn today he had pulled through.

"Meredith received two visits this morning. His first visitor was Mrs Fitt, his house-keeper. She is now back in Hyde, I am informed, making ready for her employer's return home, as soon as he should be well enough to be moved. His second visitor was Brown, the fellow who saved his life. Brown was unannounced, mind you; he seems the very soul of modesty, quite determined to shun applause. Meredith had by then fully recovered his presence of mind, and the doctor had pronounced him out of danger and able to receive visitors. But evidently the delirium was not so abated as the doctor thought, for when his rescuer entered the room, Meredith, far from showing any sign of gratitude, flung an oil-lamp at the poor man and called aloud until the churchwarden came running in to see what was amiss. This strange behaviour was all the more unexpected as Meredith is known

9

throughout his village for a kindly, restrained, well-mannered fellow. Naturally enough his outburst had its effect on his rescuer, who fled in dismay and has not been seen since."

I took another draught while I pondered what I had just heard. Try as I might, nowhere could I find any reason to suspect foul play. It was a sad affair, indeed, but one that bore all the hall-marks of an accident, not a crime, and I said as much to Holmes. He shook his head. "I think not, Watson. There is too much against it. We knew before we came here that Meredith was a local man. That, as I said, is suspicious enough. Now we have this strange business of the broken lamp –"

But I was to hear no more, for suddenly the saloon-bar door flew open and the boy from the carriage-stand ran up to announce that our cab was ready and waiting. It was time for me to make my way to Hyde.

The Ships Chandlery at Hyde was a long, low red-brick building facing the street. A yard at the back gave on to the beach. Rolls of sail-cloth were stacked in the yard, together with barrels of I knew not what, sacks piled high, and coils of rope. Deciding that nothing was to be learnt from this heap of equipment, I walked round to the front of the shop. A faded, peeling sign, scarcely decipherable, bore the legend *Ships Chandlery & Nautical Store, prop S. Meredith*, and beneath it in one small window were displayed a few nautical devices of brass. A sign on the shop door proclaimed the store SHUT, but peering through the windows I thought I could make out a figure moving inside. I rattled the door handle, to no effect; it was not until I had tapped as hard as I dared on the windows for several minutes that finally the door was opened. A neat, grey-whiskered man in a canvas serving-apron stood before me. He regretted to inform me that the shop was closed, but on my explaining that I was there to look into Mr Meredith's accident – with a hint, I confess, that my presence was of an official nature – I was admitted. We went through the shop to a small counting-house in the rear where he offered me a chair. I sat down to hear his story.

His name was Josiah Fitt, he told me, and he had begun working for old Mr Meredith, the original owner of the ships chandlery at Hyde, as an apprentice, some thirty years ago. When old Mr Meredith died, twelve years ago, his heirs, not wishing to continue the business themselves, offered it for sale. A Mr Timney, if Fitt remembered the name correctly, bought it. Timney had worked in a City bank, he had told Fitt. He had had the good fortune to be left an unexpected inheritance, and the good sense to invest it successfully, with the result that, by his thirty-fifth year, he was in a position to retire from employment. He was looking about him for a suitable place, when he heard of the Hyde chandlery being offered for sale. He came down, liked what he saw, and bought it.

People do not always take kindly to a stranger buying his way in to them, my informant told me, to which I could not but agree. Fitt assured me, however, that any resentment in the village towards the newcomer had not lasted long. The new chandler of Hyde showed himself from the first willing to fit in with the village as he found it. He even left the name of Meredith over the door, adopting, for simplicity's sake, the name of Meredith for himself. Lacking experience in the business, he kept Mr Fitt on, appointing him manager, with an increase in salary. At the same time he engaged Mrs Fitt to come in twice a day as housekeeper. Meredith né Timney proved to be a most considerate employer and colleague, and came to be universally accepted and respected in the village.

I considered that I had been given a pretty good account of Meredith, but, mindful of Holmes's injunction to leave no stone unturned, I asked if Fitt had noticed in his employer any peculiarities, anything out of the way in his behaviour or manner. Not at all, came the answer. Mr Meredith was a straightforward fellow as you were likely to meet, and, in his quiet way, friendly to all. To all except maybe the holiday folk, amended Fitt; his employer was somewhat uneasy with the crowds who came down in the Summer. But then, he added, most of the Hyde folk were of a like persuasion, himself included.

It only remained to ask if Fitt had any objection to my talking to his wife about the matter. He had none, but asked if I would forgive him if he continued his work and left me to go to the house alone and make my own introductions to Mrs Fitt. He pointed out to me his house, which was only a minute's walk away. I set off, and when I glanced back through the window I saw him take a pencil stub from behind his ear, lick it, and return to the ledger, the very picture of a village shopkeeper.

A few steps across the sunny street brought me to the house I had been shown. I pulled at the door-bell, and was answered by a matron in about her fiftieth year, of a dark, italianate colouring, with neatly dressed silver hair.

"Dr Watson, madam," I said, removing my hat. "Have I the pleasure of addressing Mrs. Josiah Fitt?"

"Oh,' she gasped, "What has happened to Mr Meredith, pray?"

"No, Mrs Fitt, I bring no news of Mr Meredith," I answered. "But I am enquiring into the circumstances of his recent accident, and your help would be inestimable. I have just spoken with your husband at the shop. Would you have the kindness to spare me a few moments yourself?"

"You'd better come in, sir. In here, if you please," she added, opening the door of the parlour. Noticing her apron and her busy air, I suggested that if she preferred to continue with her work, I would be happy to sit in the kitchen with her. "If you wouldn't mind, sir. Then I can carry on with the peas as we talk." So into the kitchen we went. I sat on a wooden chair in the corner, and Mrs Fitt resumed her seat at the table. Before her on the table stood a large pile of full pea-pods and a basin.

She leaned forward, with a smile on her kindly face and a pea-pod in her hand:

"Now, Dr Watkins, what do you want to know about poor Mr Meredith?"

I asked her if there had been anything out of the ordinary in Meredith's behaviour in the days before his mishap.

She shook her head. "No, sir. Nothing of that sort, I'm sure."

"And sea-bathing – is that an unusual thing for him to do?"

"Oh no, bless you. Mr Meredith is not a man to sit all day at his desk. Every morning he takes his constitutional before opening the shop, and likewise in the evening. Rain or shine, it makes no difference to him. Many is the time I've seen him at evening after his work is done striding out into the rain in his oilskins, and he'll come back hale as you like, ready for a good hot supper."

"And he is an habitual swimmer in the sea too?"

"He is. Not every day, and not in the winter months, of course, though there are some who do, but on a summer's day he would think nothing of swimming in the sea an hour or half-an-hour, perhaps, in the morning, or especially he likes to bathe in the heat of the day while Josiah keeps shop."

"He is a strong swimmer, then?"

"Yes – not when we first came here, mind you; in those days I would look out the back window and there he was, poor man, splashing and floundering in the waves like a fish in a landing-net!" Mrs Fitt smiled at the memory. "But he persevered, and now he slips through the water like an eel."

"Mrs Fitt, does it strike you as remarkable that a swimmer as strong as he should have come to difficulties?"

"It did surprise, me, sir, when I heard. But then the sea roundabout here is so treacherous, even for a strong swimmer, and the Blore Sands is the worst of all." Mrs Fitt looked me in the eye. "Everybody here knows the Sands for what they are. The tide comes in so fast over the shallows that a soul can find himself marooned, there on a flat with the sea running in all around him. That's where they drown, you see. With the sea up to their breast and the flat under their feet, they think themselves safe, but when the sea reaches up to their chin, and the waves lift them off their feet, they fall into a panic, and in their fear they strike out to reach the shore. But then off the flat, they find its another matter. Those channels run deep, with the sea rushing along in a flood, and it sweeps them off and away, like a twig down a stream. Why Mr Meredith chose to swim there in the Bay, of all places, I

14

cannot imagine."

"Where did he normally swim, then? Did he have a favourite place?"

"Yes, sir, that he did. He swam here in Hyde; you could see him from the chandlery window. You see, Whitsea itself is so crowded in the summer, and besides, most of the beach there is reserved for the ladies. After Whitsea, and before Hyde, are the Sands – the Blore Sands, I mean – and nobody much will swim there, so here is best, as well as being close."

"Yet yesterday he swam in Blore Bay. I wonder why?"

"Well, as I say, sir, I don't know why. A breakwater marks off the Sands from the waters of Hyde, and I've never before known Mr Meredith swim on the wrong side of it." For the first time in our interview Mrs Fitt stopped shelling peas. She put her pea-pod down and leaned forward. "This side is the safe side, they say. But I've never been so sure of that. The flats and shallows here are so treacherous; a storm may come and shift the sand and make new currents and rip-tides where nobody saw them before. So, you see, where are the safe beaches? There isn't a furlong of coast from Felixstowe to the Wash that's truly safe – that's my opinion." Mrs Fitt shook her head. "I've always worried for Mr Meredith, swimming as he does. And now this happens." With a sigh she picked up her pod and resumed her work.

I went on to ask her about the rescue attempt of the previous day, but she had not witnessed anything herself. As far as she had heard, Meredith had gone into the sea at Blore Bay, where there were very few people on the beach, and nobody nearby, except, luckily, Mr Brown. He must have seen Meredith in trouble and had gone in to help him. Meanwhile Mr Meredith's cries and splashes had drawn the few people walking on the sand into a small crowd at the water's edge. Eventually the rescuer had had to give up, and swim back to shore. At first he had wished simply to return to his lodgings. He had not wanted any fuss made over what he had done, saying it was no more than any other man would have done. A coastguard soon arrived on the spot, however, and insisted on checking the man was unharmed. His good health established, and his particulars left with the coastguard, the modest Brown retired to his lodgings in Whitsea.

We had both finished our allotted tasks: my questions were answered, and Mrs Fitt's peas were shelled. I thanked her for her help and made my farewell. Outside my driver was still waiting in the shade of a tree, and we drove back to Whitsea as briskly as we had come.

The Swan Hotel, Whitsea, where Holmes and I had arranged to meet, was an old inn furnished with a fine modern portico. On entering, I found myself in a lobby crowded with holiday-makers. Some sat in armchairs and settees, some were booking in or booking out at the mahogany reception desk, and some stood in family groups with their luggage and straw hats and shrimping-nets, while in and out among them scurried maids and waiters and porters. I was a long time seeking Holmes amid the crowd before finally I saw him at the far end of the lobby, behind a veritable jungle of potted palm, fern, and aspidistra, watching like a leopard through the foliage. I made my way through the throng to join him on the settle. As I recounted what I had learned that morning he listened with closed eyes, giving no response save an occasional nod of the head. "All much as I expected," he said when I had finished my resumé.

I was not a little disappointed at this reception. "I am glad that my morning's work has enabled me to tell you what you already knew."

"It has done more than that, Watson. It has confirmed what until now I only suspected. Of what use to me is mere suspicion? Knowledge is what I need, and thanks to your researches I have it. My own researches, on the other hand, have not been very fruitful."

From the Railway Tavern, Holmes told me, he had gone first to the sexton of St Olaf's, and was in turn directed to the doctor who had attended upon Meredith. The doctor confirmed that he had been summoned last night to St Olaf's church hall, where Meredith lay. The patient was exhausted and in a slight fever, but had not in the doctor's opinion inhaled water or fully lost consciousness for any length of time. The likelihood was therefore that he had been swept out to sea in a weakened condition, and kept himself afloat until the tide and his own efforts had brought him ashore. He had two contusions on the head, probably caused by being dashed against a rock.

When Meredith's identity was discovered, early in the morning, Mr and Mrs Fitt, being those who knew him best, were promptly informed. Meredith was not known to have any family. Mrs Fitt came to see him in the church hall, and once it was established that he was out of danger, she returned home to prepare for his return. Shortly after she left, Brown, the rescuer, came in. The churchwarden's account to Holmes of that meeting, and of Meredith's strange behaviour, did not differ from that given to me by Mrs Meredith.

Holmes leaned back on the settle. "We have collected most of the information we can, I think. Brown's recent visit to the church hall left no trace, beyond the splinters of the lamp flung at him, and naturally two tides have effaced all footprints left in the sand at Blore Bay yesterday. Those footprints may indeed have had a story to tell, Watson. A strange story, of the two men entering the sea and the one returning. However, for all that some gaps in our intelligence remain, little by little the picture becomes clearer.

"There remain three people who might throw more light on this affair: Byrd, the man who found Meredith lying on the beach; Brown, the rescuer; and Meredith himself. I fancy that Meredith, who knows most, will have least to say. Would you care to pay a visit to the man Byrd who stumbled upon Meredith? In the meantime I shall see if I can find the elusive Mr Brown. Perhaps he will have something interesting to tell us. Then, I think, the time for enquiries will be over, and it will be time for action. This affair is coming to a crisis, Watson. Death has almost struck once, and I have little doubt that it will threaten again. We must be vigilant."

I was still unable to follow my friend's reasoning. "Perhaps the heat is making me more than usually slow, but I cannot see where the dangers and complications lie. Surely the case is quite straightforward: a drowning accident has been narrowly avoided, and the man who had cheated death is now past danger and safely on the way back to health."

"You know the facts as well as I do. Do you truly think it all so straightforward? Consider the broken lamp, Watson. Consider Timney's change of name. Consider his bathing at Blore Bay, and the contusions on his head.

"I must leave you to ponder these matters at your leisure; for the present, we are not at leisure. We must finish our enquires here post haste and return to Hyde. Meredith must not be left unguarded."

"Of course, Holmes. I put myself at your disposal."

"Thank you, Watson. Your help is invaluable. Try to locate, if you would, this fellow Byrd. He lives in a cottage by the western end of the jetty, near the fishermen's chapel. Afterwards, follow on to Hyde, where we shall meet."

I had no difficulty in finding Byrd, who was at home in his cottage, but my interview with him added little to what we already knew. He told me that he walked with his dog Dodger across the sands at day-break or earlier every day, and that the previous day, before it was well light, Dodger, running ahead, had found what appeared to be a dead seal washed up on the sand. On coming closer, Byrd saw that it was the body not of a seal, but of a man. He was standing before the corpse, wondering what to do, when it got up onto its hands and knees. This alarming turn of events decided him to call for help, and he hurried along the beach to where some fishermen were preparing their boat for the tide. One of them went into the town for help, while Byrd returned to watch over the drowned man. He was soon relieved of his watch by the fisherman, accompanied by the sexton. The two men took the drowned man away on a makeshift stretcher. He had said nothing, nor made any sign, Byrd assured me in response to my questions. When I was satisfied that there was no further information to be had, I left the old fisherman and his dog in their cottage, and headed back in a four-wheeler to Hyde.

There I met Holmes as he arrived on foot, having walked along the shore from Whitsea. As we approached the chandlery, we compared our findings. Holmes's results were even more meagre than my own. He had failed to find Brown, the man who had tried to save Meredith from the waves; and when I asked him if he had learned anything from his walk along the Blore Sands, he answered only that the entire stretch of coast consisted of a great deal of sand, and nothing else.

We knocked on the chandlery door, and Mrs Fitt admitted us. Mr Meredith was lying on a wooden chest, fitted out as a kind of day-bed. A thick blanket lay over him, and his temples were bandaged.

"Now if you gentlemen will excuse me, I have work to do," said Mrs Fitt. "I shall be in the scullery if you need me." The door closed behind her.

"I am pleased to see you back in your home, Mr Meredith," said Holmes. "You already appear much improved since this morning in the hospital. This is my friend and colleague Dr Watson, who is assisting me in this matter."

Meredith stretched up his hand. "How do you do, Dr Watson? I am grateful to you gentlemen for having taken an interest," he continued, "and I am relieved that the matter is concluded. I don't wish to be inhospitable, but complete rest is what I have been prescribed, and I that is what I shall have until my health is returned. My housekeeper will see to that."

"Very good, Mr Meredith," answered Holmes. "There are one or two aspects of this matter which are still unclear to me, however. Will you be kind enough to satisfy my curiosity on a few points before we leave you?"

"I shall do my best."

"What did Brown strike you with?"

Meredith looked astonished. He opened his mouth but no answer came.

"Come now, you must surely have noticed."

Meredith found his voice, albeit querulous. "I cannot understand you. The gentleman did his best to save me from drowning." Anger gathered in his pale face, and he pointed a shaking finger at Holmes. "I have a question for you, though. Who are you, you and your friend here? And by what right do you come here and poke your noses in my affairs?"

Holmes smiled. "I admire your spirit, Mr Samuel Meredith or Timney, but it won't do. To answer your questions:- I am Sherlock Holmes, the private detective, and my friend and colleague here is Dr Watson, late of the Indian Army. We poke our noses into your affairs, my good sir, in order to save either you or your old acquaintance from murdering the other. Before we go any further, Mr Meredith, let me make one thing clear to you. It may help to put your mind at rest. My colleague and I are here as private citizens, no more. At present the police are not involved, and if this matter is cleared up satisfactorily, there is no reason why they should be."

Meredith stared up at Holmes, anger, confusion and fear contending for expression on his face.

"Do not distress yourself by further denial, I beg you," continued Holmes. "Perhaps if I put the facts before you, you will understand that the game is up. You will tell me if I go wrong at any point in my account."

Holmes drew up a chair close to Meredith's day-bed and began his narrative, counting off each stage of the story on his fingers.

"Twelve years ago you came here in an attempt to start your life anew. You were successful. At first you lay low, but as the years went by you began to feel more secure. Then yesterday, as you came out of the sea from your morning swim, you were suddenly confronted by a face from the evil days of your past. This Brown – I shall trouble you for his true name a little later – is a dangerous man, and he was armed. The two of you walked along the shore towards the Blore Sands, he holding his pistol. When you reached the Blore Sands he forced you at pistol-point into those treacherous waters. He followed, and you fought in the waves. Two blows to the head blacked you out, whereupon he pushed you out into a rip-tide. As you were being swept out to sea, Brown swam back to the shore and passed himself off as a would-be rescuer.

"When you came to, you found yourself out at sea and moving further out in a strong tide. But you had strength enough to save yourself from drowning, and eventually you fetched up on the shore, more dead than alive. They carried you to a sick-bed where you were nursed back to health. But the horrors were not over. As you lay helpless in bed, the man who had tried to kill you came into your room. In fear for your life you threw the lamp to keep him at bay and shouted until someone came in, and he had to leave.

"Is there anything in my account you would like to correct?"

Poor Meredith could only answer with a helpless shrug.

"Do not lose heart, I beg you," said Holmes. "Things look black, but we may yet win the day. I have some hopes that we will be able to apprehend this fellow Brown."

"But Mr Holmes," groaned Meredith, "if he is apprehended, I am ruined. Once the police come to hear of this matter my past is discovered, and my life here at

Hyde over."

"Precisely, and that is why it must be we who apprehend him. I do not anticipate any need to alert the police force, and Brown himself is hardly likely to go to the police."

Meredith hesitated still.

"Come, we have little time. You are in the gravest danger, and the crisis is fast approaching. Brown will not let the grass grow under his feet. Every hour he waits is an hour in which, for all he knows, you may talk to the police, and he find himself arrested on a charge of attempted murder. Only when your silence is ensured will he feel safe. He will act quickly, therefore. It is probable that he will make his third attempt on your life tonight.

"You may choose to decline the help Dr Watson and myself offer you. But understand this: if we are not here to help you, the police will be."

Meredith started and put up a hand in protest.

"No, no, Mr Meredith. You would give us no choice. A murder is likely to attempted – the attempt may well succeed. Can we stand by in silence while you are murdered?"

Meredith thought the matter over in silence, then slowly nodded his bandaged head.

"Very well, Mr Holmes. You offer me Hobson's choice. Indeed, I don't mean to sound ungracious. I do not think I could be in better hands, after all. I had thought my past, and what happened yesterday on the beach, was a secret known to no-one but myself and Brown, but now I find you know everything. I had better have a man like you on my side than against me. I accept your help, Mr Holmes, and gratefully."

"Very good. Now, tell me this: did Brown come after

you here deliberately, or did he come across you by chance?"

"It was pure chance. He was taking a holiday at Whitsea and happened to see me. He asked here and there, and found out where I lived and worked. I had often wondered in the back of my mind if such a thing might happen one day."

"And what was the reason for his attack? Did he try to try to blackmail you about your past? Was he after some treasure or money from the old days?"

"In part he was after money, yes. He drew his pistol and insisted on coming back with me to the shop, and threatened to expose my past if I did not pay him. But it was not just a question of money. The truth is, he was a brutal, vindictive man, and to see an erstwhile mate who had turned his back on him and the old ways made him furious. He was in a rage, as well as in a lust for gain, and when he pulled out his pistol I feared for my life."

"I see. You were between the devil and the deep blue sea, and you chose the sea.'

"That's about it, Mr Holmes. But little good it did me, for the devil came after me anyway. He closed on me in the waves, and struck me such a couple of blows on the head that I blacked out." With a rueful grin Mr Meredith lightly touched the bandage round his head.

"And you could not expose him, without exposing your own past. By the way, what is his real name?"

"Beasley, Ned Beasley."

"Thank you. Now, we must prepare for this evening. You came here in a cab, in full public view. Beasley probably knows you are here; that is all the more reason to expect him tonight. We must be ready for him. Can you trust your man Fitt?"

"Absolutely."

"We will need his help. Tonight Watson and I will wait here for your visitor. Beasley must suspect nothing, for if he once smells a rat, he will be gone. And although it may be days before he returns, return he will. You cannot live with such a threat over your head, Mr Meredith, nor defend yourself against it. Let him come tonight, when we are ready and can prepare for his attack.

"Have you ever known Beasley use a rifle?"

"Never. A pistol was always his weapon."

"Very well. We will presently ask Mrs Fitt to go home and to send Mr Fitt back here to the shop. He will make what arrangements are necessary outside the premises. Watson and myself, I need hardly tell you, cannot risk being seen. We are the teeth of the trap, Mr Meredith, and you are the bait. You will lure Brown, or Beasley, here. It is a dangerous game we play; are you prepared for it?"

"Indeed I am, Mr Holmes. I will not be bullied by that villain."

"Excellent! Now, the success of our plan hinges upon Beasley's being persuaded that you are quite unconscious of danger. Only then will he attempt to strike; and when he does, we will have him. This is how we will proceed. While daylight continues, you may make yourself conspicuous in the house. Do not venture too close to the windows, for if you present a clear target he may take a shot at you. Further from the windows you will be safe, for he will not fire with a pistol at an uncertain target. He has failed twice in his attempts on your life, and was doubly lucky to escape arrest; he knows he cannot risk failure again.

"It will be a warm night; we may credibly allow

ourselves to leave open a window. I believe I smell cigars, Mr Meredith – Cuban, if I am not mistaken. You are a smoker?"

"You are right, Mr Holmes, I am, but in my present state of health . . ."

"I dare say Watson or myself could be persuaded to be your substitute in the matter of smoking a cigar," smiled Holmes, "if I do not presume too far on your generosity. I do not know how well Beasley is acquainted with your smoking habits, but in any event, the aroma of cigar smoke floating out into the night air will surely suggest to him that his prey is lying within, at ease and unaware of danger."

Mr Meredith smiled in return. "Of course, Mr Holmes and Dr Watson. The box is over there behind the counter. The fourth shelf down."

"You are very kind. To return to our plan: what rooms are there upstairs?"

"There are three rooms: my bedroom, on one side of the landing, and on the other side two smaller rooms."

"No other room on the same side as yours? No bath-room, or dressing-room, perhaps?"

"There is a kind of lumber-room or annexe off my own room."

"Does it have a door on the landing?"

"No, it can only be reached through my own room."

"Then it is safe, and you will sleep there tonight. This is the plan: when the sun sets, Fitt will close the shutters and leave for his own house. In your bedroom the lamps will be lit and the curtains closed. At ten o'clock we will turn out the lamps down here and move upstairs, you to sleep in the lumber-room, and Dr Watson and I to lie in wait for Beasley."

There was little for us to do then but to lie low and wait for darkness to fall. I watched the seagulls circling slowly over the sea crying, or settling on the roofs of Hyde. As the sun began to set, Fitt came back to do what was necessary outside the house. He worked alone, as Holmes and I durst not risk being seen. All but one of the shutters on the downstairs windows he closed, and that remaining one he left not properly fastened from within; a blade slipped between the two shutters would lift the bar, and the shutters would be open. Meredith assured us that to Beasley, this was as good as to find the front door wide open. (Neither of us needed to press Meredith further on the nature of Beasley's criminal past; as Holmes somewhat acerbically remarked to me later, to guess it was within even my deductive powers.) While I locked the upstairs windows thoroughly, Fitt dragged the ladder that lay in the yard into the shop, laying it on its side along a wall. Once he had locked the back door, preparations on the outside of the building were complete. He locked the front door, and with a loud "Goodnight, Mr Meredith," spoken for the sake of any ears that might be listening in the dark, he walked off to his house.

Inside, we went upstairs to Meredith's bedroom and arranged bolster and pillow to resemble a figure in the bed. We then checked on the lumber room where Meredith was to pass the night. It was a windowless room, more secure than comfortable, equipped with a camp-bed that brought back to me memories of my Afghan campaign. All was now ready upstairs. We closed the curtains and went back down to the shop, where we lit the lamps and settled down to smoke and wait.

We thought it safer to pass the evening in silence,

conversing, where necessary, in signs, for outside in the dark Beasley might be circling the house, listening, or trying to peep in through the windows. We had noted the lines of sight offered to a prowler by the peep-holes in the shutters, and calculated which parts of the shop were safe for us to use, not being visible from outside. The restrictions on our speech and freedom of movement became extremely irksome, and even when we did move, we must needs take unnatural paths in order to avoid the forbidden parts of the shop and its little back parlour. It was most strange to see Holmes shuffling around the room sideways to escape being seen, his back to the wall, or ducking low, below the line of sight, swinging along with bent knees like a great ape in the gaslight. I dare say I presented as risible a figure as he. As for Meredith, it would have been no disadvantage for him to be visible from without, but being too weak from his ordeal to move about much, he was content to lie stretched out on a bale of sailcloth behind the shop counter. So we sat or lay there, unable to converse, limited as to our movements, each of us alone with his thoughts.

When the time came, Meredith signalled goodnight and went upstairs to his cabin-room.

Holmes and I remained downstairs a little longer. In whispers we rehearsed our plan. We were to lie in wait in the bedroom, Holmes's station being by the door, on the hinge side, so that when opened it would hide him, and mine behind the wardrobe that stood on the other side of the doorway.

If Beasley did come, we would hear his entry and be ready for him. We would allow him time enough to approach the bed, but not to realise that the bed was empty, for once apprised that something was wrong, he would immediately be on his guard. We would strike first, before he could take alarm. Surprise, speed and darkness would be our allies.

It was an hour since Meredith had gone upstairs. We stood in absolute silence for a full minute, straining our ears for the least sound. We could hear nothing. Creeping low, we extinguished the lights and went upstairs to adopt our positions.

"Ready, Watson?" Holmes whispered.

"Ready."

"Good luck!"

I felt my way round to the other side of the wardrobe, and put my cocked revolver upon its top. As the minutes passed, my eyes accustomed themselves to the darkness, and the room took form about me. The dressing-table seemed slowly to materialise, and upon it a wash-bowl and ewer. Then a small chair became visible, and over the bed the dark rectangle of a picture. Once I leaned forward from behind the wardrobe to see if I could make out my friend. I could just distinguish his upright figure.

The hours crawled by. Who knows what are the strange noises in a house at night? I had time enough to wonder what they were. There were creaks that made me freeze and listen for another step, little scratchings and taps, and once human-sounding groans from close by – Meredith, no doubt, in some fearful dream, perhaps a dream of drowning. All of a sudden from outside the house a cackle broke out. Was it Beasley who had disturbed the sea-gulls? In a few minutes their squabble died down and silence returned. Twice, approaching steps from the street made me hold my breath, and twice they passed by and away into silence.

It seemed to me increasingly likely that we had

misjudged the situation, and that Beasley was not going to come to the chandlery that night. Why should he? Surely, having failed to kill Meredith, he would go back home and ponder his next moves in safety. If he was really as black as Holmes painted him, that is; perhaps indeed Holmes had been entirely wrong, and the whole affair was merely what it had appeared to be, a tragic near-drowning. But no, for Meredith had confirmed Holmes's account. My mind was beginning to wander. I was tired, I realised, and needed to keep my wits about me. To that end I decided to recite silently to myself the names of the muscles of the human body I had learnt as a medical student, starting with the head: *occipitofrontalis, occipitalis, frontalis,* I remembered, *orbicularis oculi, corrugator supercilli, depressor supercilli . . .*

There was a noise downstairs. An even, gently rasping noise, as of something sliding. The shutter bar! Then followed a long silence. I was wondering if perhaps I had imagined the sound when it was repeated. It was followed this time by a click, then, after another pause, by the sound of two surfaces rubbing together. I silently leaned forward to see the dark shape of Holmes. We exchanged a sign. He had heard too.

Footsteps crossed the wooden floor below us, and an occasional creak marked their passage up the stairs. When they reached the top I could hear the rustle of clothes as somebody moved stealthily along the landing. The steps stopped outside the door. I held my breath. The door opened a few inches, and stopped. Then, slowly, it opened wide into the room. A figure glided in. It stood facing the bed for some seconds, then moved forward. At that point Holmes with a shout of 'Now!' leapt from behind the door, lashing downwards. I seized the arm and neck, and between us we forced the struggling figure to the floor. He continued to writhe and thrash on the boards until he felt my revolver pressed to his ear. He froze in fear and lay still, panting.

"The game's up," said Holmes clearly. "Do you have him safe, Watson?"

"I do."

Holmes rose and lit the lamp. "Take a chair, Beasley," said he.

I motioned our captive to his feet and over to the chair. As he moved into the gaslight he was revealed as a well-knit man of some thirty summers, his handsome features disfigured by a sneering expression. Holmes kneeled and reached under the dressing-table to bring out Beasley's pistol from where it had fallen in the struggle. "Loaded, I take it?" asked Holmes, cocking the hammer, and Beasley's involuntary start informed us that indeed it was.

The lumber-room door opened and Meredith entered the room in a dressing-gown. He and Beasley glared at each other, but exchanged not a word.

"Good morning, Mr Meredith," said Holmes. "I apologise if we disturbed your sleep. Please be seated.

"Now, Ned Beasley," he continued, "I am undecided as to what to do with you. I have grave doubts about the wisdom of allowing you to remain at large. However, your old friend Mr Meredith has reasons of his own for not wishing to call in the police. Before I decide which course of action to take, I shall let me lay some of the facts before you, so that you may understand your own position.

"Myself and my colleague here are aware of your past association with Mr Meredith, and of your attempts on his life, first on the Blore Sands, and then this morning in the church hall. We are witnesses to your third attempt just now."

"As to that, it's your word against mine," came the surly response.

"Indeed. And whose word will the judge and jury believe?"

Beasley shuffled his feet and made no answer.

"I continue. The three of us here have enough information against you to send you to gaol for a long term. Mr & Mrs Fitt will be provided with sealed letters to take to the police should any unfortunate accident befall Mr Meredith, and in that unhappy event Mr Meredith's executors will find a similar letter. Even a man of your limited understanding will think twice before committing any more murderous attacks, I think.

"Of course, you may think fit to take the fight to me," said my friend, and he tucked a card into Beasley's breast-pocket:

SHERLOCK HOLMES

221b Baker Street
London WC

"I shall always be pleased to receive you."

Dawn was breaking as Holmes and I walked back to Whitsea across Blore Bay. The tide was out, revealing acres of gleaming sand. Pools and rivulets of tidal water glittered in the early sun, and fainter in the distance glittered the ocean itself. Over our heads gulls floated and called, occasionally flapping down to the sand to peck at some stranded creature of the deep.

"I still cannot understand how you puzzled it all out, Holmes. You promised me an account of how you did so."

"Did I, indeed? How rash of me. Well, if I wish to be considered a man of my word, I had better oblige.

"As you know, the circumstance that immediately aroused my suspicion was that it was a local man who had drowned, or, as it turned out, nearly drowned. The newpaper correspondent seemed think that, as drownings were lamentably common at this spot, another was not suspicious."

"I must confess that I thought so too."

"Whereas in reality," continued Holmes, "the more notoriously dangerous the place was, the more unlikely that a local man would willingly go bathing there. What induced him to go into the water, I did not then know, but I already suspected that something was wrong.

"I then considered the rescue attempt. How did we know that that Brown tried to rescue Meredith? I asked myself."

"But that was public knowledge, Holmes. It was reported in the paper. There were people on the beach that morning, who all saw what happened. How did you ever come to doubt it?"

"You know my methods, Watson; I make no assumptions, and consider every possibility. The little crowd on the beach; did they really see what happened? At a distance of perhaps one or two hundred feet, the words and faces of two men struggling in the sea would be unidentifiable. How could a bystander know who had been doing what to whom? Brown came out of the sea saying he had tried to save a drowning man, and the crowd believed him. They accepted that an attempted rescue was what they had just seen. But that 'rescue' was a mere unsupported claim made by one of the two men, and one that fitted the facts less and less well as they came to light.

"Let us move on to another part of the puzzle, and consider the question of our man's name. Meredith, we call him, as does everyone. But as you discovered, that is not his name. Why did he change it?"

"We know that from Josiah Fitt, if you remember," I replied. "It was mere convenience; he took that name from the name of the business he bought. It was already written over the shopfront."

Holmes waved away my answer. "Come now, Watson, are we really to believe that? When you took over your present practice, did you adopt the name of its previous owner for the remainder of your life? Of course you did not. You did what anyone else would have done, and proudly put up a brass plate with your own name upon it. Here was Timney, if that was his name, making a new start in life, with enough ready money to buy the business outright; why did he not go to the signwriter, and have his own name, new and shining, over his shop, for all the world to see? Why did he leave the old peeling sign there, as if the shop had never changed hands, and even take the old name for his own. Why?"

"He wished to leave his old life behind him."

'Well, yes, so he did, but there was more to it than that, Watson. After all, a man may leave his old life behind him without going so far as to change his name. No, Timney's behaviour was unmistakeably that of a man who not only wished to retire from his old life, but to hide it. He did all he could to ensure that Timney vanished from sight for ever, to be replaced by Meredith.

"Next comes a very strange episode. When the modest hero of the beach visits the recovering Meredith he is met with an astonishingly hostile reception. Meredith flings a lamp at him and cries out until help comes. Why did Brown's visit strike such terror into Meredith's heart? It was becoming harder than ever to believe in Brown's bona fides as the well-meaning rescuer.

"It became harder yet to believe in them when the doctor told me of the injuries to Meredith's head. How did he come by them?"

"Surely they were made when the waves dashed Meredith onto some rocks?"

"What rocks?" was my friend's reply, as he indicated with a sweep of his hand the expanse of sand we were crossing. From Hyde to Whitsea, and from the distant sea on one hand to the grassy dunes that marked the margin of the beach on the other, there was not a rock to be seen.

I had one last question for my friend. "You seemed quite sure that Beasley would break into the chandlery last night. How could you be so certain? I will confess, Holmes, that many times last night I thought we had misjudged the situation, and Beasley would never appear."

"My dear fellow," he laughed, "you were not alone. I too was far from certain that Beasley would come; it was a gamble, and more than once last night I wondered if the gamble had failed. You are quite right, Watson: it was perfectly possible that, both his attacks on Meredith having misfired, Beasley had given up, and left Whitsea, so that while we lay in wait for him in the bedroom of the chandlery, he was far away, asleep in his bed. But, after all, the gamble was worth it. What did we stand to lose? A night's sleep. And how likely was it that Beasley would give up and go home? His nature argued against it; he was a violent, vindictive man. His situation was against it too. He had twice attempted to murder Meredith; if he stopped now, he would be leaving alive and resentful the one decisive witness against him. Meredith was the one who knew his real name, knew his old haunts and comrades – knew enough to have him tracked down. While Meredith lived, Beasley was not safe. My instincts told me he was still here in Hyde, out there in the dark, desperate to break in and finish the bloody work he had started.

"Well, the gamble paid off, and I think we may be content enough with the outcome of our little adventure. Beasley may be a vicious dog, but even a dog, once thoroughly beaten, accepts defeat. He will slink away snarling with his tail between his legs, and leave Meredith to continue his quiet and useful life as the ships chandler of Hyde."

We had come to the western end of Blore Bay. Ahead of us appeared the town of Whitsea, lit by the early sun, the spire of St Olaf's rising above the roofs of the houses. Holmes and I turned back to look at the sands we had crossed, unearthly in the raking light, our footprints trailing away into the distance back towards Hyde. Soon they would be washed away by the incoming tide.

Holmes clapped me on the shoulder. "Come, Watson, our work here is finished. A well-deserved breakfast awaits us at the Swan Hotel, and then the train back to London."

The Glebe House Affair

IN STORING THE MANY documents relating to the career of my friend Sherlock Holmes I have been assiduous enough, but in organising this mass of material I have been less thorough. The contemporaneous reports, the mementoes, and the press cuttings are all flung into the strong-box until such time as they may be reduced to order; but, inevitably, that time seldom comes. The demands of daily life will not be ignored, and as the days and weeks pass into years, these papers lie unsorted and forgotten. It is a state of affairs with which Holmes himself seems to be entirely contented. He has never evinced the least interest in his old cases for their own sake, a nostalgic regard for the past being entirely foreign to his cold and unsentimental nature. Indeed, I am convinced that he would be happy enough entirely to abandon his past cases to oblivion, were it not for two considerations: the first being a certain egoistical pride in his work, and the second, the usefulness of these records; for it has sometimes happened that the circumstances of a past case have cast light upon a present enquiry. One such occasion arose only yesterday, when Holmes, busy on a case of great urgency, asked me to find for him the records of an enquiry he had conducted long before into the *Jenny Lind* and its unusual cargo. I went upstairs, delved deep into the box, and eventually dredged up from its depths the case-papers he had demanded. As I drew them out, a foolscap envelope that had become entangled with them fell out. I picked it up from the floor. The words GLEBE HOUSE were written upon it; it was another case entirely, unconnected with the mystery of the *Jenny Lind*, but something prevented me from immediately dropping it back into the box. 'Glebe House' – the name brought back memories of an adventure I had shared with Holmes many years ago. Once I had handed Holmes the records he had requested, I returned to my desk with the Glebe House envelope. There I untied it and carefully pulled out its contents: a small sheaf of notes in my own hand, two yellowing newspapers, and a dried rose-petal. These meagre relics, now lying before me on my desk as I write, tell the story of the African adventurer Hugo Mayne, found murdered at the edge of a lake in Suffolk.

The case began one quiet morning in Baker Street. Death having brought my marriage to a premature end some years previously, I had relinquished my private practice and moved back into the flat that I had shared with Holmes in my bachelor days. If I was less inclined to be sociable than of old, and sometimes found conversation irksome, Holmes, with his monkish silences and aloof manner, was a most congenial companion to me; in difficult times, I discovered, an old friend is the best friend. We had breakfasted together that morning, and now that breakfast was over, had made ourselves comfortable, I reading a medical journal, and Holmes deep in the newspapers of the past several days. It was quite like the old days before my marriage. Two hours had passed in silence when our tranquillity was interrupted by the sound of the door-bell and steps upon the stair.

"Expecting a visitor, Holmes?" I asked. He shook his head.

There was a smart rap at our door. "Come!" called Holmes, and a gentleman of middle age, dressed in mourning, entered the room. He glanced at us uncertainly, from one to the other.

"Mr Sherlock Holmes?"

"Good-morning, Mr Edward Ayres," answered Holmes with a bow. "I am afraid the weather in London this morning is less favourable than in Suffolk. Be seated, I beg you."

So taken aback was our visitor that for some seconds he stood staring open-mouthed in silence.

"You have my sympathies for the death of your brother-in-law," continued Holmes. "It is his death, I take it, that has brought you here?"

Our visitor found his tongue at last. "Mr Holmes, you surpass your reputation. You are right in every respect. How in the name of Heaven do you know who I am and what has brought me here?"

Holmes acknowledged the compliment with a slight nod of the head. "Merely through observation, Mr Ayres, and a few simple inferences from what I observe. Your dress and bearing proclaim you to be a gentleman, and your complexion proclaims you a country gentleman. On the newspaper you carry, though its title is folded away, I see an advertisement for a Corn-chandlers of Bury St Edmunds, from which I presume that you come from

Suffolk. Your complete mourning tells me that you have recently lost a close family member, and the fact that you have come to consult a specialist in crime suggests that the death is criminal. If I add to this information what I have read in the newspapers about Mr Mayne, murdered in the grounds of his brother-in-law's place in Suffolk, who might you be, but Mr Mayne's unfortunate brother-in-law, Mr Edward Ayres?"

"You make it sound quite logical. And I suppose there is some simple sign telling you that it was not raining in Suffolk when I left?"

"Very simple signs indeed. You stand before me in a linen coat, lightweight boots, and no cape or great-coat. Is that how you dress to go out into the rain? Now, sir," Holmes continued, "this is entertaining, but we have more important matters to discuss. Please make yourself comfortable in the easy chair, and tell us all that you can about the murder of Hugo Mayne. My information at present is limited to what has appeared in the newspapers. You may speak freely before my friend Dr Watson. He has been an invaluable ally in many of my cases."

Our visitor took his seat, put his papers and hat upon the table, and plunged straight into his story.

"It is a dreadful thing that has happened, Mr Holmes, quite dreadful. My wife's peace of mind has been shattered by it. Naturally the police have been investigating the murder, but my wife and I are both of the opinion – but I find that I am running ahead of myself. Forgive me, gentlemen; my mind has been in a turmoil these last four days. I shall begin again.

"It was on Monday last, and my wife and I were in the library of Glebe House, my place in Suffolk. The lamps

40

were lit, but shutters were still open, for the sun had not long set. We were in our usual places, and at our usual past-times of that hour: Mary busy at her embroidery-work, and I reading. Suddenly in the quietness we heard a sharp report. We looked at each other. I rose and went over to the window, and looked out towards the lake, whence the noise had seemed to come. Nothing was to be seen in the thickening light. I resumed my seat, and my reading, and Mary resumed her embroidery. A branch snapping, perhaps; we thought no more of it, and soon after we went in to dine. Hardly had we taken a mouthful of soup when we were interrupted by the entry of Mottram, muddy and breathless."

"Mottram?"

"The groom. He begged for a word with me alone. I knew at once from his manner, and indeed from the mere fact of his interruption, that something grave had occurred. He and I went into the hall, where he whispered to me in a shaking voice his news; he had found Mr Mayne dead down by the lake, his skull crushed.

"I gave orders for the maid to come with sal volatile and sit with my wife, and for the boy to go to the village and fetch the police. That done, Mottram and I hurried down to the lake. As we ran through the meadow in the twilight I harboured some hope that my brother-in-law's injuries were not fatal, and that he might still live. It seemed to me that if any man could cheat death, that man was Hugo Mayne, for he had already done so once. But my first sight of the body, even in the failing light, was enough to dash my hopes. It lay on its back, the legs and his one arm flung out in the mud, and the head twisted so far round as to be facing almost upwards. The back and top of the head were staved in. I dare say you two gentlemen are accustomed to violent death in many forms, but I am not. I hope never to see such a sight again.

"I covered Hugo's remains with my coat, and we waited beside the body, Mottram and I. It grew quite dark among the trees. After what seemed a long time we saw a point of light like a star, near the village, twinkling on and off; little by little it approached; when it reached us it was revealed as a policeman with his lantern, come to stay by the body until morning. Mottram and I left him to his lonely task and returned across the field to the house.

"Upon my arrival there I was met with the news that Hugo's rooms had been burgled. I gave orders that nothing there was to be touched until the police came."

"Mayne lived in a suite of rooms in your house, I believe?"

"That is so, Mr Holmes."

"Pray proceed."

"The next morning some half-a-dozen policemen arrived at Glebe. Two of them talked with me and my wife, and then with the staff, finding what they could from us – which was little enough. The other policemen were at the lake, by Hugo's body – 'the scene of the crime,' as they called it. Once I had finished speaking to the sergeant I went down to the lake again and watched the activities of the officers there. They were busy enough; measurements were taken, the ground examined, the body sketched, and samples of I know not what put into little envelopes. I am sure you two gentlemen know a good deal more than I about what was done there. So it went on, for two hours or so. The final task, when all else was done, was to lift poor Hugo's body onto a stretcher and carry it away. Since then we have not seen the police at Glebe House."

"Thank you, Mr Ayres," said Holmes. "There are one or two small matters I should like to clear up. How long elapsed between you and your wife hearing the gun-shot and the groom Mottram telling you of Mayne's death?"

"I should say about four minutes."

"Thank you. You mention that Hugo Mayne was clutching in his hand a revolver."

"That is so."

"Did he normally carry it with him?"

"No. It was normally kept locked in his desk."

"Did he often go to the lake, or walk the grounds?"

"He was a great walker in the grounds, and beyond them, but the lake was not one of his favourite haunts. A damp, gloomy place, he called it, fit only for poets. He preferred the open fields."

"And was that the usual hour for his walk?"

"As to the hour, he was not a man of very regular habits; he walked whenever the fancy took him."

"Even at dusk or in the dark?"

"Even so."

Holmes gave a sharp nod of his head to our visitor. "You have made the circumstances of your brother-in-law's death very clear. I see you are a smoker, by the way. Would you care to try one of these Abdullas?" He pushed the cigarette-box towards our visitor.

"Thank you." Ayres lit one and blew out a fragrant cloud of tobacco-smoke.

"Mr Mayne had lived with you at the Glebe house for a long time, had he not?"

"He had been with us for twenty years."

"Were you and he friends before your marriage?"

"No, Mr Holmes, I married before I met Hugo. That was twenty-two years ago. Mary Mayne, as she then was, had no sisters and but one brother, Hugo, whom I had not met, for he lived in Africa. Mary and I had been in my place in Suffolk for a year and a half. We were happily settled there and our first child had not long been born when we received news that Hugo was returning to England. Mary was fond of her brother, but her pleasure at the prospect of being reunited with him was subdued by the sad circumstances that forced his return. He had been mauled by a lioness; one arm was already taken off, and a leg so severely bitten that it was in doubt whether he would ever walk again."

"Poor fellow!" I exclaimed. During my time in India I had seen such injuries caused by tigers. They usually proved fatal.

"Indeed. It must have been a ghastly business. It was on a lion-hunt; his gun jammed, and the brute was on him in an instant. His fellow hunter shot her, but terrible damage had already been done. Mayne's arm required immediate amputation. When he was sufficiently recovered to travel, he was brought back to England. Naturally I invited him to stay at Glebe House until he should recover his health. That at least is how I expressed it to my wife; but having heard the extent of his injuries I privately thought it as likely that he would be coming to Glebe to die in the old country. In either case, I thought, he was welcome to come to us. Come he did, and we were all astonished at how quickly his health returned. Within a few weeks was hobbling around the grounds at a great pace, nothing daunted by his horrific injuries. When he had gained as much of a recovery as he ever could, and begun to set his business affairs in motion, my wife and I decided to invite him to stay on as a tenant. It seemed a natural step to take; Hugo liked the place, Mary was pleased to have her brother close to her, and I liked the fellow, and was pleased to have an addition to the estate's income; and so it was agreed. He became a permanent resident of Glebe House, and so he remained until the dreadful events of last week."

"You say that Mayne had only one arm, and one leg severely damaged."

"That is correct."

"I am surprised, then, that he was such an enthusiastic walker."

"Mr Holmes, we were all surprised. As I say, we expected an invalid, a broken man, come home to die. Nothing could have been further from the truth. His resilience astonished us all." Sir Edward shifted his look away from us and he slowly shook his head. "Poor Hugo! I can see him still, stumping across the fields on his stick, his chin foremost."

"He walked alone?"

"Not always. He often walked accompanied; by a guest, or a friend. Often by the Mottram the groom or by the dog."

"His walking-stick – was it by the body when you arrived there?"

"Yes, lying near him."

Holmes picked up from the table the newspapers our visitor had brought, and quickly glanced over them. "Can you tell me what progress the police have made in their inquiries? Have they made any advances on what is set out here?"

"Unfortunately, very little progress has been made. At any rate, they have not apprehended the culprits."

" 'Nothing was found in the murdered man's pockets,' "
Holmes read aloud from the newspaper. "That is surely
an exaggeration. Nothing of value, they probably mean. I
do not suppose that the thieves troubled to take his
pocket handkerchief."

"Well, you must ask the police inspector that, Mr
Holmes, but I was told that nothing at all was left on his
person."

"Hmmm. And they consequently take the view that Mr
Mayne was set upon by some local ruffians, the motive
being robbery. Is that your view of the matter?"

"I am not a detective, Mr Holmes. It is your view of the
matter I have come to hear."

Holmes smiled. "Nevertheless, I should be interested
to hear what you think."

"I suppose a casual robbery is the likely explanation,
and that seems to be the view taken by the police. But my
wife and I have some doubts. There has never been any
trouble in our part of the county from the kind of villains
who would do such a thing. Poachers trouble us
sometimes, of course, and there is the occasional scuffle
among fellows returning from a long evening at the
public-house in the village. As a magistrate I am
accustomed to such outbreaks of unruliness, and I would
not claim that our corner of the county is the Garden of
Eden; but nor is it the Jago. We are not brutes who would
smash in a man's skull for a few pounds.

"That is my story, Mr Holmes. My wife and I seek
justice for Hugo Mayne. We are not satisfied that the
police are doing all that can be done. If it was indeed a
local man who killed Hugo, we want that man found and
brought to justice. If it was not, we must know what really
lies behind this cruel murder."

Ayres paused, as if wondering whether or not to speak out. Suddenly the words welled out: "My wife loved her brother, Mr Holmes. They were orphaned as children. In the cold and distant household to which they went, they had only each other to cling to for warmth and affection. You will understand that she feels his death very keenly, very keenly indeed. I try to comfort her, but I find that I cannot. She will not rest until we know the truth."

Holmes rose to his feet. 'Thank you for bringing the death of your brother-in-law to my attention, Mr Ayres. It presents a number of singular points, which incline me to the view that you and your wife take; that although it may seem at first sight to be a simple robbery, there are signs that robbery hardly comes into it, and that we are dealing with an extremely complex murder. Its apparent simplicity may be an effect that has been deliberately created in order to draw attention away from the true nature of the crime. I shall be pleased to look into it for you."

"I am very glad to hear you say so, Mr Holmes."

"I will call upon you at Glebe House tomorrow morning, if that is convenient. Good day."

Once our visitor had left, Holmes lit another cigarette and sat for a while in silence, gazing unseeing into space. The dreamy, far-off look in his eyes was a sign, long familiar to me, that he had withdrawn his attention from his present surroundings and was concentrating his thoughts elsewhere.

He put out his cigarette. "I am not sanguine about the chances of success, Watson. The scent is cold. Still, there are points of interest. The fact that the Mayne was armed is suggestive, is it not? And the fact that nothing was found in his pockets. And, indeed, the fact that he went down to the lake at all. How are you fixed, Watson? Are you able to leave the practice for a day and come down to Suffolk tomorrow? I should value your help."

The following morning Holmes and I took the train to Suffolk. At the station a four-wheeler was waiting to take us to Glebe House. We jogged along at a lively pace through the quiet lanes until we came to a drive with a small lodge on the corner. In we turned and drove more slowly along, raising a swirl of dust behind us. To our right lay meadows, and on the left a lawn edged by topiary trees in the formal, stilted manner of a hundred years ago. We followed the drive where it lay between an avenue of majestic old cedars, leading to a great stone gateway whose pillars framed our first view of Glebe House. Bushes of rhododendron on either side led down to the front of the house. There we were admitted and shown into the morning-room, where Edward Ayres and his wife greeted us. Mrs Ayres was a handsome lady, silver-haired and very pale in complexion, the whiteness of her face made more striking by the black of her mourning. Her manner, though polite and graceful, was distrait, as if her thoughts were elsewhere.

Holmes wished first to visit the lake where Hugo Mayne had been found. The groom Mottram, who had discovered the body, was appointed to be our guide. We found him waiting for us outside the front door, the same man who had just driven us from the railway station. He led us through the formal garden, whence we jumped down a ha-ha and crossed the field that led down to the lake. The lake was crossed at its narrowest point by a mossy stone bridge, and Mottram pointed out to us where, near the foot of the bridge, he had found the body. Holmes quickly looked about him, darting here and there, examining the broken branches of bushes and the bloodied leaves, getting down on all fours to peer at footprints in the damp earth, inspecting the path and parapet of the bridge, and looking into the water.

"Have you found anything out, sir?" asked Mottram.

"I have found out that a herd of policeman recently passed this way, trampling everything in its path," came the reply. "I do not think there is anything more to be learned here. Let us return to the house."

As we made our way back, Holmes chatted with the groom about the dead man. Mayne did not keep a horse of his own, we heard, but he occasionally rode with the hunt on a mare of Ayres, and was, despite his injuries, a fearless horseman. He was an occasional visitor to the stables, exchanging information of varying reliability with Mottram about forthcoming races. Both men liked a modest gamble, and Mayne often carried with him a hip-flask from which the two, and the stable-boy if he was there, would celebrate the outcome of their bets or find solace for them. Holmes asked our guide to show us Mayne's apartment. We were led to the ground floor of a tower, a later addition to the original building, built on to one side of the house, with large French windows facing the garden. The groom opened the French windows for us and then left us to examine for ourselves what had been Mayne's home for the last twenty years of his life. In we went; and in stepping over the threshold, I had the sensation of stepping into the dark continent itself. Native trophies, antelope-hide shields and assegais adorned the walls. A sinister *fetisch* figure stood upon the desk, and the desk itself stood upon a lioness-rug, glass-eyed, the lips curled back in a snarl to reveal discoloured fangs. A basket in the corner, fashioned from an elephant's foot, bristled with umbrellas, walking-sticks, knobkerries and a sheaf of spears. Holmes looked around him and threw out his arms in a gesture of despair. "What am I to do here, Watson? Everything has been tidied away since the burglary. Any signs as to what happened here have been systematically destroyed, first by the local police and then by the maid." He turned to the French window. "Let us hope that we can at least see how they entered." He took out his magnifying lens and examined minutely first the edge of the door frame, and then the door itself, turning the key in the lock to and fro. "No fresh scratches on the strike plate or the bolt," he pronounced. "The burglars did not have to force an entry."

"You mean that Mayne left the window open when he went down to the lake to meet his death?" I asked.

"Either that, or the intruder had a key." Holmes fell to looking over the room's contents, the trophies on the wall, the papers, the books in the small book-case, the walking-sticks, searching everywhere, it seemed, for a clue, and, to judge from his reaction, finding very little. For want of anything else to do I glanced through some of the books. They told the same story as the spears and knobkerries, the story of years passed in the untamed wilds of Africa.

"Anything of interest there, Watson?"

"Nothing unexpected; 'Early Travels in South Africa', a medical guide, that sort of thing. Here's a book of poems - 'Songs of Sentiment'. What are these pinkish wafers between the leaves? Oh, I see, they are old rose-petals. And there's an inscription on the fly-leaf: 'Hugo Mayne, from F.C.' Well, so the old adventurer had a softer side, once!"

Holmes gave a snort of amusement. "Well done, Watson! I can always rely on your keen nose for an affair of the heart. Have the goodness to ring the bell, will you? I should like to talk with the maid."

A homely woman of advancing years answered the call. She was the housekeeper for Mr Mayne's apartment, she told us. The staff had been sitting down to their dinner that fatal evening when the boy was called upstairs. He came down to tell them of the murder before running off to fetch the police. She, accompanied by the footman, had gone straightaway to Mayne's quarters, and found them in chaos. She had only half an hour earlier prepared Mr Mayne's dinner-table for when he should return from his walk; now all was in a state of utter disarray. In the largest room, which served as sitting room and study, the desk had been ransacked, its drawers pulled out and emptied onto the floor. The little locked drawer containing Mayne's revolver was unlocked and empty. Mayne had no safe in his rooms; she supposed he kept his documents and valuables in his London bank (a supposition later confirmed by Ayres). For all the mess they had made, the thieves had not found much to take beyond a box of cigars, an ivory paper-knife and a wallet containing, no doubt, some bank-notes and coins. The house-keeper was not able to say how much money, but as Mr Mayne was a gentleman who enjoyed a wager, she supposed it might have held as much as thirty pounds. As for the rest of Mayne's apartment, the bedroom had also been entered, to much the same effect; the wardrobe doors stood open, and the contents of the bedside cabinet emptied onto the floor, but nothing was missing. So it was with the kitchen; cupboards had been opened and jugs and cups inside them knocked over, drawers had been pulled out, but nothing was taken except a carving knife. Holmes wondered if the intruders might have taken some small item whose absence the housekeeper had missed, but she was quite firm that it was not so; she had been housekeeper to Mr Mayne for sixteen years, she told us, and knew every single item in the suite. He then asked about Mayne's usual habits, and in particular about his gun and his movements about the grounds. He had no rifle, a useless item to a man with only one arm. His revolver was always kept locked in the top drawer of his desk. He never normally carried it; the only time she could remember his having done so was years before, when a violent gang of house-breakers had terrorised the neighbourhood. At that time he had taken his pistol with him on his evening walks; when the gang was broken up, his pistol went back into its drawer. As for the evening walks, they were regular but unpredictable: regular in that he was an indefatigable walker, and unpredictable in that there was no pattern to his walks, no time or route that he favoured. He might walk before dinner, or after; he might walk alone, or with Mungo, the dog, or with Mottram the groom, or with a guest, if he had one. He might walk around the fields and circle back, or go down beyond the lake to the village and take a drink or two with friends or strangers in the public-house before returning home. The one unchanging constant was that he walked. If a day came that did not see him stumping jauntily somewhere about the grounds, it was likely to be a day of one of his periodic visits to London.

Holmes's final question concerned several cases of wine which stood in the kitchen. They had arrived that very morning, we were told, and in the confusion and upset caused by Mr Mayne's death had not yet been taken down to the cellar. Holmes glanced at the delivery note accompanying them; it listed wines of the highest quality, and a correspondingly high price, from a vintners in St James's. Did the housekeeper know how and when they had been ordered? They must have been ordered, she thought, about ten days earlier, when Mayne had gone down to London. He had stayed there overnight and returned the following day in excellent humour, bringing with him several boxes of the best cigars, and telling her to expect a delivery soon of some fine Burgundy and Champagne wine. He had even brought back a box of bon-bons for her, she added, the memory of his act of kindness obliging her to dab her eyes with her kerchief. What had occasioned this sudden *largesse*, she could not say; she could only guess that perhaps Mr Mayne had been lucky at the horse-races. Holmes had been sitting quiet during the housekeeper's account, throwing out an occasional question when further elucidation was required, but otherwise suffering with remarkable patience the many digressions in her narrative (digressions which I have omitted from my summary of her testimony). Finally he thanked her for her help, and she, wishing us God-speed with our search for Mayne's murderer, returned to her duties.

For some minutes after she had gone Holmes sat brooding, in his grey eyes the dreamy look I had learned to associate in him with extreme mental concentration, his brow furrowed as he brought into focus some difficulty that eluded solution. He spoke his thoughts aloud. "Something happened," he said. "Why did he suddenly have all that money to spend? Why did he go down to the lake, where he never normally went? Why did he carry his revolver? Something happened to bring about these changes. What was it?" He leapt to his feet. "No good sitting here trying to spin out theories on insufficient data. More information is required, Watson. Perhaps Edward Ayres will be able to supply it. Let us search him out!"

We found our host in the library, where he invited us to join him. The library of Glebe House was a vast room, three of its walls covered by dark, deeply-carved bookshelves that rose to the frieze of the ornate plaster ceiling. In the middle of one wall was a stone fireplace, above which hung the portrait of a bewigged man with his hand resting on the pommel of his sword. The room was lit by a pair of unusually high bay windows in the opposite wall. I was seated by one of these windows, which afforded me a fine view of the grounds, from the parterre, in which a gardener was working, to the field down to the wooded lake where Hugo Mayne had met his death, and beyond the lake to the village with its church spire and the distant plains stretching away to the horizon.

"Are you one of the executors to your brother-in-law's will, Mr Ayres?" asked Holmes.

"I am."

"I should like to see his cheque-book together with a statement of recent payments, if you have one."

"Your luck is in, Mr Holmes. As executors we demanded full statements of account from his bankers." He went to an escritoire, unlocked a drawer and took out a sheaf of papers. "They are somewhere here . . ." he said, leafing through them. "Ah, these are they!" He handed the papers to Holmes.

"Thank you. Just the last month's figures should be enough." Holmes glanced down the columns. "I find no mention here of any payment to the vintners who supplied the wine that arrived for Mr Mayne this morning. Nor any cheque made to them," he added as he flicked through the cheque-book. "Do you know if he had an account with them?"

"He did not."

"And no recent payments into his account, I see. Did he have another banking account, do you think? Perhaps in a different name?"

"I think not, Mr Holmes. We have uncovered nothing of the sort in his papers, and I can see no reason why he should have one. My brother-in-law was not a secretive man."

"I see. That is curious. No cheque drawn on his bank, no account with the wine or tobacco merchants, and yet he bought himself cigars and wines fit for a king."

"Indeed he did, and not only for himself. He gave me a box of Havanas, and my wife a handsome muffler."

"Paying ready cash for all these things, evidently. Can you account for this sudden liberality?"

"Liberality from Hugo needs little explanation. He was an open-handed man. As to where he found the money, that is more difficult to say. My guess would be at the race-track."

"Ah, his housekeeper was of the same opinion. Now," said Holmes, settling back in his chair, "I must ask you to cast your mind back over the last month or so, if you would, and tell me of any unusual circumstance that comes to mind, in particular anything that might pertain to Mr Mayne. Did he receive any visitors? Did he make any visits himself?"

"He had no visitors that I know of, no. But he did go away to London at the end of the last month. He stayed for one night. That was two days before he was found dead."

"Do you know where he stayed?"

"He always stayed in his club."

"Which was his club?"

"The Capricorn."

"Were such visits unusual for him?"

"No. He visited London perhaps half-a-dozen times a year. He had both friends and business interests there."

"I see. And in the main house; did you have many guests or visitors? Anything out of the usual way of things?"

"Very little, Mr Holmes. We lead a quiet life here. Friends to dinner occasionally, of course, mostly neighbours. Hugo joined us for many of those evenings. But they were nothing out of the way – quite the opposite. Our guests were all old friends, people we had known for years.

"At the beginning of last month we held a luncheon-party, as we always do, in the garden and library. The weather was fine, luckily. Hugo was there, of course. Not that he stayed for very long. He went back to his own suite early, and I can't say I blame him. The whole thing became somewhat of a bore, to be honest. We see pretty much the same old faces every year."

"No newcomers at all?" asked Holmes.

"Oh yes, one or two. General Wallace, a widower. Indian Army, retired now. He has just moved down here, and we thought we ought to invite him. One doesn't want to be unfriendly. Our new member of Parliament, of course, Bonnington Smythe; he was here, though his wife could not come. There was a Varsity friend of my son – I hadn't seen him before, and don't much mind if I never see him again – and some people called Blaine." For a few moments Ayres scoured his memory. "I think those were all the new people we've had here recently, Mr Holmes."

"Thank you." Holmes stood up. "We have taken up enough of your time. I think my researches can now better be pursued in London."

"I trust you are making some headway, Mr Holmes. May I know what theories you have developed?"

"It is not my business to develop theories, Mr Ayres, but to discover the truth. The truth of what happened to Mr Mayne is beginning to emerge here and there from the mist, but much is still hidden. You may rest assured that if I do discover the truth, you shall know of it immediately."

We returned to the station, leaving, as we had come, in the carriage driven by Mottram. As we rattled along, he and Holmes engaged in a discussion of the merits of the runners at the next meeting at Newmarket. Mottram favoured us with what he assured us was a 'warm' inside tip. He had already had some money on the horse himself, he told us, at excellent odds.

"I hope you are as lucky as Mr Mayne was the other week," said Holmes. "I hear he quite cleaned out the bookmakers."

"First I heard of it!" came the answer.

"Ah," said Holmes, "but perhaps he kept his luck to himself."

"Perhaps he did, sir. Perhaps poor Mr Hugo kept quiet about a win at the races, and likewise, perhaps hogs might fly."

Holmes laughed. "Well, he had some wind-fall, did he not? I wonder what it was."

"Couldn't tell you, sir."

"He said nothing about it? That sounds unlike him, from what I've heard of the man."

"Well, as a matter of fact he did say something, but what it meant is a mystery to me. This was just before he went to London that last time. He talked about some buckshee that was coming his way. It had been due nigh on twenty years, he said, and now the time had come at last. And if you can tell me what he meant by that, sir, you're a wiser man than I."

We had arrived at the station. "Well, Mottram, here's some buckshee for yourself," said Holmes, handing the groom half a guinea.

"Right you are, sir. Thank you." Mottram pocketed the coin, whipped up the mare and rattled down the road back to Glebe House a good deal faster than he had come.

We arrived in Baker Street early in the evening. Holmes strode immediately to the bookcase, hauled out a volume and spread it before him on the table.

"Now," said he, "let us see what we can find out about these newcomers to Glebe House." He lit the lamp and turned it up high, hovering over the tome like a bird of prey. "General Wallace . . ." He flipped through the pages. "Here we are! 'General Sir Robert Vansittart Wallace, DSO, etc.' " Holmes read the entry briefly in silence – "No, I don't think the General can help us," he concluded. " 'Blaine' was another name. Let me see . . . no, no Blaine in here. Unless it's spelt otherwise . . no. I'll try the MP, Bonnington Smythe. He was the other newcomer." Holmes read out the entry:

" 'SMYTHE: Captain Robert Algernon Bonnington, MP, born 1858, son of . . .' Ah! This is better; 'Matobo expedition," he read, "1878(despatches); Administrator for Matabeleland, 1885; contested Birmingham South, 1892; MP North Kensington, 1895; Under-secretary to the Foreign Office, 1896; Colonial Secretary – ' and so it goes on.

"Well, Watson, that is interesting, is it not? The young Bonnington Smythe was in Matabeleland at the same time as Mayne."

"Mayne was in Southern Africa, at any rate," I ventured.

"In Matabeleland. Did you not see the inscription on one of his sticks? 'Hugo Mayne, Matobo, 1879.'"

"Ah! Better still!" Holmes suddenly exclaimed. "Listen to this: 'Married Florence, youngest daughter of Revd. Henry Charteris.'"

"I don't quite see . . ."

"The inscription in the book of poems! You found it yourself, amongst Mayne's books. In the fly leaf, you remember? 'To Hugo Mayne,' it ran, 'F.C.'"

"This is excellent!" cried Homes, his eyes glinting. "The mists begin to clear. A definite picture emerges of the background to the Mayne killing. That is fortunate, for I have other calls upon my time which cannot wait much longer. A strange, back-to-front sort of case, is it not, Watson? When the crime of twenty years ago is perfectly clear, but the crime of last week is still shrouded in uncertainty. Perhaps one day you will favour the public with an account of it; it should suit your story-telling method.' He glanced at the clock. 'Half past five o'clock. There is still time to visit the Bonnington Smythe household. I am tolerably sure as to the events behind the murder, but it is as well to be certain, and an interview with Bonnington Smythe, husband or wife, will establish the facts beyond doubt. Will you accompany me,

Watson?"

"Alas, I cannot. I have an appointment."

"Very well. I wish you a pleasant evening." He seized his hat and hurried out.

When I returned that evening, eager to hear about his visit to the Bonnington Smythe home, there was no sign of Holmes. The next morning he was already gone, or still sleeping, and I breakfasted alone. So it was that evening, and so it continued for the following five or six days. Where he was, and what cases he was working on, I had no idea. But although I had lost touch with Holmes, I had news enough of Mr Bonnington Smythe, almost every morning in the newspapers. Courts require proof and certainty before they punish the guilty, but for society, suspicion is enough, and it was evident that the deepest suspicion hung over the head of the eminent politico, for every day brought news of some fresh humiliation as one by one his powerful friends turned their backs on him. It was reported that upon rising to make a speech in the House he was greeted by booes and hisses, from his own side of the House as well as from the benches opposite. Ugly rumours concerning him were circulated in the press, and in some papers his name began to be openly mentioned in connection with the Hugo Mayne murder. Then it was announced that he had been relieved of his cabinet responsibilities. So the spate of reversals continued, until finally it became evident that his public life was ruined beyond the possibility of recovery.

One afternoon at his time I returned to our flat to find Holmes seated in his armchair, leaner than ever, and brown as a nut. He looked up from his newspaper and greeted me with a casual nod of the head. I was eager to hear from him about the case whose public aspect had so dominated the political news for the last week. "My dear fellow," I exclaimed, "I am delighted to see you. Have you got to the bottom of the case?"

"Yes, yes, it was Maratin, the Viper of Montpellier. It was the rope used to raise and lower the basket that gave him away."

"No, I mean The Mayne murder."

"Oh, that. No, I have not. It is most disappointing. Nothing from the Baker Street irregulars, and nothing from the official force either." The irregulars of which he spoke was the squadron of well-trained street urchins who, at the princely rate of a shilling per day per urchin, would search out vital scraps of information inaccessible to more formal bodies. Holmes had instructed them, and his underworld contacts, to keep their ears and eyes open for any signs as to the identity of the hired killers of Mayne. He had also approached the police inspector in charge of the case, advising him where to look. He had even spoken to his old friend Lestrade, who was not officially concerned in the case at all, for Lestrade, though limited in his acumen, had the virtues of thoroughness and tenacity in full measure. For the past week, while Holmes himself was on the continent, these agents had continued his enquiry. "It is strange that nothing has turned up, Watson," he said. "How can it be that after a week of searching by so many agents, official and otherwise, not a single clue has come to light? There can be no doubt that Smythe hired two or three thugs to kill Mayne. Is there not somewhere a message from Smythe, a witness who saw him with the murderers? Has there been no rash act by the killers, no mistake to give them away? I begin to suspect that Smythe was not alone in this plot. I sense an *eminence grise* behind this affair, someone more cunning and professional in arranging an assassination than friend Smythe could ever have been. This casts a different light on the problem. If my suspicions are right, then there is little point in wasting more time in searching for clues, for there are none to be found.

"Of course the outlines of the case are perfectly clear, but mere outlines are not enough. Until we have our hands on the perpetrators of the crime I cannot regard the matter as resolved."

"I'm sorry to say that even the most rudimentary outlines of the case are far from clear to me, Holmes. I should be grateful if you could sketch them out for me."

"Throw me the tobacco, Watson, and I will be happy to satisfy your curiosity." He put a match to his pipe and drew, until clouds of smoke began to billow and rise. "The first thing that brought itself to my attention," he began, "was the nature of the crime itself. The attack upon Mayne and the burglary of his quarters were most accurately coördinated. Consider the timing; Mottram found the body of Mayne immediately, for he came tell his master within four minutes or so of the gunshot, yet the murderers or murderer had already vanished without trace. Mayne's rooms were ransacked before the arrival of the housekeeper and footman, but they arrived at Mayne's quarters a mere five minutes or so after the gunshot. All had been well only some twenty minutes earlier when the housekeeper had set the table. Either the burglars did their work quickly and hurried down to the lake to kill Mayne, or, more likely, there were two parties – the burglars and the killers – working almost simultaneously. In any event it was clear that we were dealing not with a crude crime of opportunity, as the police supposed, but a carefully planned stratagem. The element of burglary was interesting; little of value was taken from the flat – objects that might have been seized almost at random, inconceivable as the intended haul of a robbery – and yet the place had been thoroughly ransacked, and Mayne's pockets utterly emptied. Why should that be so? Evidently the culprits were not seeking valuables. What, then? Presumably something that would incriminate –perhaps something suggesting a motive for the murder, perhaps a note giving a rendezvous – who knows? The possibility of an incriminating rendezvous note, by the way, was given a little more weight by the place of the murder. The Glebe House lake was not a usual resort of Mayne's, but, being comparatively isolated and half-hidden by trees, it would provide an ideal spot on which to kill the man, if only he could be lured there. Very well; we have not a common burglary that led to a fight, but a deliberate, carefully planned murder. A murder carried out, in all probability, by strangers, for local men capable of such violence would surely be known and suspected. Only in a city would such desperate characters be able to lie low.

"We now come to the victim. I was immediately struck by the circumstance that shortly before his death Mayne's customary behaviour changed in several small ways. He started to carry a gun; he visited London – that was not so unusual in itself, but when there he spent profusely, and spoke of coming into funds that were long overdue. On the evening of his death, his walk took him to a place where he seldom went. If there were any lingering suspicions that his death was a commonplace theft gone awry, these unaccounted oddities of his behaviour dispelled them. Something had happened to bring about these changes in his ways. What was it?

"The answer to that question came when I looked up the details of Bonnington Smythe, the recent visitor to Glebe House. It was immediately obvious that here was the missing piece in the puzzle. Bonnington Smythe had been in the same part of Africa, and at the same time, as Mayne. He had married Florence Charteris; was she the 'F.C.' who had given Mayne a book of love poems? Mayne had spoken of his windfall as having been overdue twenty years; that is, it dated from his time in Africa. From all this it was evident that the story began twenty years ago, in Matabeleland."

Holmes shot a glance in my direction. "You will tell me, Watson, if I fail to make clear the logical sequence of thought I describe?"

"So far I follow you perfectly, Holmes."

"Excellent. Let us agree, then, that the changes in Mayne's behaviour derived from his meeting again this person from his past. That raises the question: what was the nature of their friendship? Already, with the book inscribed from F.C., there is the possibility that twenty years ago they were rivals in love. And if Smythe and Mayne contested for the young lady's affections, it was remarkably convenient for Smythe, was it not, that Mayne should suddenly suffer a dreadful accident?

"I shall return to that in a moment, but I wish first to address the subject of money. On his visit to London Mayne flung money around with abandon, buying gifts for one and all, himself included. Where did the money come from? To rephrase the question: what happened in Africa that twenty years later produced for Mayne such buckshee, as he called it, and why did he think it his due?

"So we have these two separate things; the events in

Africa, and the sudden windfall of money. I put them together, and asked whether Mayne's mauling by the lioness was connected to his windfall of a fortnight ago."

"There you lose me, Holmes," I interrupted. "How could they be connected?"

"Well," said he, "it could be that Bonnington Smythe had some guilty part in the accident; that twenty years later, at the Glebe House garden party, Mayne recognised his old rival; that he confronted him, and Bonnington Smythe paid him off."

I was speechless as the enormity of the suggestion sank into my mind. Holmes, imperturbable as ever, said nothing, merely knocking out his old briar in the grate and refilling it.

"My suggestion seems to have shocked you into silence, Watson," he said eventually.

"I don't mind admitting that it has. Are you saying that Bonnington Smythe deliberately engineered the accident?"

"I don't say that he did, no. I say that it is a hypothesis that covers all the facts. Can you think of another?"

I could not. Staggered though I was by my friend's conjecture, the more I turned it over in my mind, the more probable it seemed. Young men, in a wild and lawless country, are capable of much, both of good and bad. Smythe, it seemed, had turned to the bad; perhaps in the end his vile act of treachery, committed all those years ago, had indeed come back to haunt him.

"And you suggest that Mayne exacted money from his old friend? That is little short of blackmail, Holmes."

"Well, perhaps so, if you care to look at it that way. I doubt if that is the way Mayne looked at it. His old friend, as you call him, had deprived him of his arm, half his leg, his sweetheart, and nearly of his life. Mayne would surely have seen any payment he might extract from Bonnington Smythe as perfectly justified reparation. His due, as he put it to the groom."

"That would explain the money that suddenly came to Mayne, I grant you; but what about the murder?"

"The murder follows on naturally from the picture we have already built up. Bonnington Smythe paid once, but he realised that he might have to pay again and again, and, worse, that Mayne, a wilful, loose-tongued sort of man, might, in his cups, let the cat out of the bag anyway. In that case, even if the matter were never to come to court, the scandal would mean the end of Smythe's career – as indeed it has. He decided there was only one thing for it; to silence Mayne for ever.

"Well, the Right Honourable Robert Bonnington Smythe is scarcely the man to spill the brains of another with his own hands. He is a man of the world, a man with contacts; a word in the right ear, and the men to do his dirty work for him were found."

"Good Lord! The man is a minister of the Crown. It's an ugly story, Holmes."

He shrugged. "Ugly stories are my speciality."

It was a masterly synthesis of the facts. Yet there was a doubt in my mind, which I could not pass over in silence. "I dare say you are right, Holmes. It all fits together. But where is the proof of what you say? What evidence is there?"

"Well said, Watson! You are quite right: it was all mere supposition. There was, however, an obvious way of testing it, at least as far as the events in Africa were concerned. I could ask Mrs Bonnington Smythe, née Charteris, to see how much of my hypothesis was true.

You remember I went to the Smythe London home in Lowndes Terrace last week, when you had other commitments. Let me tell you about that visit, Watson. Smythe was not at home, and I sent in my card to the lady, with a note that I wished to speak to her about the death of Mayne. I was admitted to a small first-floor room, where I had not many minutes to wait before Mrs Bonnington Smythe entered. She was a well-made woman, five feet four inches in height, firm in character, and although expensively dressed, neither wasteful nor given to vanity. As soon as I saw her I read in her face that she knew of Mayne's murder. No doubt she had read of it in the newspapers.

"I informed her that I was retained to look into the murder. 'You and your husband were friends of Hugo Mayne in Africa, I believe?' I asked.

" 'We were.'

"I explained that it was necessary to ascertain some personal matters about the past in order to form a right view of the case. I told her that I had seen the book of poems that she had given to Mayne. She looked at me and nodded assent – it was she who had given him the book. I needed to go further:

" 'Forgive me, Mrs Bonnington Smythe; was Hugo Mayne a suitor of yours in those days?'

"Again she nodded a silent affirmation.

" 'Thank you. Now, if you would, please tell me about the lion-hunt in which Mr Mayne was injured. Pray do not omit any detail.'

"She took a few seconds to compose herself. Her lips trembled, but she held firm. Still standing, her hands resting on the back of a chair, she told me her story.

" 'Our party comprised myself, my father, Hugo and

Robert, together with the servants and bearers. We camped out for two nights. I had been on a hunt in the bush before; we would set up camp where the scout thought lions were to be found, and the men would go off into the bush for a mile or two with a couple of Africans, taking a kid as bait.' "

" "Was it not dangerous for you to be left behind, unarmed, with lions at large?' "

" 'I never thought so for a moment. The rest of the Africans were with us. They could keep off any lion with noise and fire. Or perhaps it was merely the thoughtlessness of youth that made me feel safe.

" 'The first day was unsuccessful. On the morning of the second day, father was unwell. He decided to stay behind with me while Robert and Hugo went out on their own. They were preparing for the hunt in their tent, and I went to wish them luck. As I approached the tent I heard Robert's voice through the canvas. "It's all right, old boy," he said. "I've done yours too." The two men walked out for about two miles. We could see them far away, tiny figures in the distance through a haze of heat. They tethered the kid, took up their places and waited. For a long time nothing happened. Eventually I joined Papa in the tent, out of the sun. I had not been in the shade of the tent long when suddenly we heard in the distance a terrible cry. We rushed out. A lioness had one of them in its mouth, shaking him like a doll from side to side. The other figure hesitated what to do, then fired, but the shot seemed to have no effect. He fired again, and again, and finally the beast dropped her victim and tried to run away. He shot again, and she fell. By now I could tell which was which: it was Robert who had fired, and Hugo who had been mauled. He lay on the ground, quite still.

We all rushed over to the scene, of course. My father fitted tourniquets to Hugo, who was bleeding dreadfully. A stretcher was made from one of the tents and the party returned to the town as quickly as possible. Hugo was given what care he could be given. His arm was amputated.

" 'Father and I were due to return to England within a week. It broke my heart to leave Hugo in that state, but I was given no choice. I visited Hugo each day before we left, of course, but he did not regain his consciousness. With Papa I left Matobo and returned to England, to our home in Wiltshire. I wrote regularly to Hugo, but I never received a reply. I wrote to Robert, too, asking about Hugo, but had no reply from him either.

" 'It was not until some years later, when father was very ill, that I was visited by Robert in England. Those terrible events in Africa I had never forgotten, of course, but they had faded into memory. You understand, I am sure; in time the pain gradually lessens, and is replaced by a kind of sadness. Robert had done well in Africa and was pursuing a political career in England. Hugo had died, he told me. I was deeply saddened by the news, but not surprised. Robert continued to call on me. He was no longer a youth; he seemed older by more than the few years that had passed since the African days. Even his name was different. In Africa he had been plain Robert Smythe.

" ' "It's Bonnington Smythe now," he said. "One needs a name that will stand out from the crowd at Westminster. Sounds well, don't you think?" He had become a man of the world, and I was still only a girl. Within three months we were engaged to be married.'

" 'There is one detail of your story I would like to

confirm with you,' I said.

"She looked at me steadfastly. 'I know what it is,' she answered. 'It is the words I heard outside the tent, on the morning of the accident.'

" 'That is right.'

" 'I am absolutely certain of what I heard, Mr Holmes. Let me explain to you. At the time that I heard those words, they meant nothing to me. I never thought of them for a moment. Until last week, I was unaware even they were in my memory. Then, when I read the papers, and realised that Hugo had been alive all this time, the past came back to me. I remembered those times in Africa when I was just a girl, excited by the novelty of it all, and I remembered Hugo, and Robert as he was then, and most of all I remembered that last hunt. Every detail of that day came back to me, and one detail in particular has haunted me. I have heard those words so many times in my mind these last few days. It was just as I told you, Mr Holmes. I was walking between the tents, and as I approached Robert and Hugo's tent I heard Robert's voice coming from inside. I can hear him now; "It's all right, old boy. I've done yours too."

" 'You have understood the import of those words, Mr Holmes, have you not? Robert must have been talking about loading the guns. It was he who prepared Hugo's gun – the gun that failed to fire.'

" 'Have you any idea as to Smythe's motives for such an act?' I asked her. 'Was it rivalry with Mr Mayne for your affections?'

" 'I'm not sure if it was my affections he longed for, or my inheritance,' she answered bitterly. 'Father's health was frail, and the doctor had warned him that he was unlikely to reach old age, a warning that I was rash enough to repeat to Robert. My mother died when I was an infant, and I was their only child. At father's death all he had would come to me.' "

Holmes had smoked out his pipe, and leaned forward to knock it out in the hearth.

"So there it is, Watson. My reconstruction of events, as far as it went, was confirmed by the lady's testimony. But the most important question of all – who killed Hugo Mayne? – remains unanswered. The police, the irregulars, all of them have been trying for a week to find the answer, and have found precisely nothing. There is only one thing for it, Watson. I must beard Smythe in his lair."

He looked at his half-hunter. "Five o'clock. I believe there is a debate in the house tonight, is there not?"

I consulted the Times. "Yes, upon bi-metallism and the gold standard. 'The value of the rupee,' " I read, " 'and hence the oeconomy of India, is the subject– ' "

"Never mind the subject of the debate," Holmes interrupted. "When will they vote?"

" 'The debate is not expected to continue late.' "

Holmes sprang to his feet. "Then I had better go there immediately."

"Would my presence be of help?"

"It certainly would. He is as as slippery and lethal as a cobra, this fellow. Remember your Shakespeare?" he continued as we hurried down the stairs. "*We have scotched the snake, not killed it.*" A wounded beast is the most dangerous, Watson. We must be on our guard."

When we arrived at Westminster the debate was still in progress. We had as our guide a clerk, provided for us by a Member of the House whom Holmes had helped in the past. The fellow soon established that our quarry was not

71

in the debating chamber, where he was now a figure of derision, and accordingly took us to Smythe's office, but he was not there either. Our guide suggested the Whips' office, but there we learnt that Smythe had that day lost the party whip. He had reacted to this latest disgrace with anger, and stormed out of the office hardly an hour ago. The opinion in the office was that it was unlikely that Smythe was still in the House.

"This smacks of desperation, Watson. They won't have him in the chamber, they won't have him in the Whips' office – he is running from one bolt-hole to another, but they are all stopped. Where can he go now?"

"He cannot rely on a welcome at his clubs," I answered. "Except his own home, I cannot see –"

"Precisely, Watson! His own home. Come, it is not many minutes distant."

Holmes and I hurried out of Westminster Palace and struck out along Victoria Street, and thence through Grosvenor Gardens and Eaton Square. So brisk was my companion's pace that I could scarcely keep up without breaking into a run. "Smythe's place is at the further end of the street," explained Holmes as we turned into Lowndes Terrace. "Hulloa! What's this?"

A constable was stationed at the steps to the front door. Holmes ran up to him: "Good evening, constable. We are here to see Mr Bonnington Smythe."

"It's Mr Holmes, isn't it? If you'd be good enough to knock, someone will let you in."

A butler opened the door to us. There was a ghastly look about the man; his face was the colour of ash. Holmes handed him his card and announced himself: "Mr Sherlock Holmes, the detective." The butler glanced over our shoulders at the constable on duty, who gave him an affirmative nod.

"Of course, sir. You wish to see . . ."

"That is why we are here."

The butler admitted us, and walking down the hall, opened a door. He ushered us into a darkened room, turning away from it himself with a shudder. We passed him and stepped inside. The heavy curtains were drawn closed, shrouding the room in such a gloom that at first I could hardly make anything out. It seemed to be a dining-room in the grand style. From the ceiling hung an enormous glass chandelier. The walls were dark and hung with paintings. As I took a step further into the room I recoiled, for I felt the carpet beneath my feet to be sticky. Beneath the long dining-table which occupied the centre of the room I made out, as my eyes accustomed themselves to the darkness, something lying on the carpet, covered in a sheet. A dark stain marked the sheet at one end. Holmes knelt down and lifted it at the stained end. He looked carefully at what lay beneath, and then silently replaced it. Standing up, he crossed the room and drew back the curtains, and as light flooded into the room the full horror of the scene was revealed. Daylight revealed the stain on the sheet, that I had thought black, to be red, the brilliant scarlet of arterial blood. It had spread in a pool across the carpet to where I stood, and away in the other direction beyond the table. As an army surgeon I had become accustomed to the sight and smell of blood, but I had known it on the field of battle; in this refined and splendid setting it had a new power to shock, as it squelched in the carpet beneath my feet or dripped slowly from the dining-table. Blood seemed to be everywhere; it had even sprayed over the lower pendents of the chandelier. The man, having severed an artery, must have staggered about the room, spouting blood as he went, before collapsing to the floor. A carving-knife lay on the carpet beyond the table. "What an end to a brilliant career," said Holmes as he looked about him. "What would Mayne have said, I wonder, had he known that the man who ruined his life would end by taking his own? Well, we can do nothing here. Smythe has gone, by his own hand, and noone in this world can harm or help him now."

And so the case of Hugo Mayne's murder came to its bloody and unsatisfactory end. The murderers were never brought to trial for their crime. As for Robert Bonnington Smythe, though he escaped the arm of the law, he can hardly be said to have escaped justice. His suicide caused a brief public scandal, after which his renown sank without trace. It might truly be said that for his crimes he forfeited both his life and his fame. Who now remembers the name of the man once hailed as the rising star of his party, and a future Premier of his country?

The Case of the Vanishing Fish

WHEN I MARRIED and set up privately in Paddington, my wife and I moved into a house near my new surgery, and I abandoned my old friend Sherlock Holmes to the sole occupancy of the Baker Street rooms we had once shared. The unsettled life of my bachelor days was replaced by the comforts of marriage and the regular employment of a busy medical practice. It was a happy period of my life; intrusions upon my domestic contentment were not, therefore, likely to be welcome, least of all if they chanced to come just as I had settled comfortably at home after a taxing day's work. Thus it was that when one evening a telegram arrived for me as I sat at dinner, I so far forgot myself as to slam down my knife and fork, and ask if a fellow could not be left to dine in peace.

The message that had so angered me ran thus:

MEET TOMORROW AT ALL SAINTS COLLEGE
= ROOM IN FOUNDERS RESERVED FOR THE
NIGHT = HOLMES +

The peremptory tone of the thing did nothing to soothe my irritation. It was typical of Holmes to send, at the most inconvenient possible hour, a telegram containing neither apology nor explanation. For some minutes I bemoaned the high-handed manner of my friend, and thanked Providence that my life was now shared with a loving wife. As I resumed my dinner, however, my indignation cooled. I was bound to admit, in justice to my erstwhile companion, that I had never had cause to regret my involvement in his cases. The adventures in which I had played a part could be described variously as bizarre, dangerous, or grotesque; but never as humdrum. The prospect of a new case, as I turned it over in my mind, began to appeal; perhaps the spirit of adventure was still alive in me, and stirred at this call like an old hound to the sound of the horn. Holmes was, for all his faults, the most extraordinary man I had ever known, and during these last few years, he had become a figure of national, even international renown. Yet he still turned to me, his old companion, when he wanted someone upon whom he might rely. Could I turn my back on him? So my thoughts ran on, as I ate; with the result that by the time I had finished my dinner, I was almost fully persuaded to fall in with Holmes's wishes and pay a visit to the University. The matter was finally settled by the ready acquiescence of my wife, who gave her opinion that a day or two away from the practice would do me no harm. So it was decided; and the following afternoon found me in that ancient university city, an overnight bag in my hand, walking through the narrow lanes that lead to All Saints College.

The bells of the city's colleges and churches were

chiming five o'clock as I arrived at the porter's lodge of All Saints. There I was handed the key to my room, and told that I might expect to find Professor Hendricks and Mr Holmes in the Senior Common-room. A college servant escorted me there, leading me through a small courtyard and a maze of passages whose stone floors had been worn smooth over the centuries by the feet of scholars. We arrived at a heavy oaken door, which my guide opened for me. Stepping inside, I found myself in a large and gloomy hall, its panelling made dark by candle-smoke. At the far end stood a massive granite fire-place, and on one side two long windows allowed the view of a sunken lawn. A few gowned men, whom I took to be fellows of the college, were seated in high-backed chairs, talking or reading. At the far side of the room I saw, silhouetted against a window, the familiar hawk-like features of Holmes, who was in conversation with one of the fellows. I made my way over to them.

"Ah, Watson! I knew I could rely on you." Holmes indicated his companion. "Professor Hendricks here is an old friend of my undergraduate days." The professor was a short gentleman, broad and pink of face. His eyes blinked behind thick spectacles in an expression of bewildered innocence. Though prematurely bald on the pate, his hair sprouted densely about his ears. His appearance put me in mind of a monk; it suggested a life sheltered from discomfort and temptation.

"The professor here is one of your readers," continued Holmes. "I thought you might be interested in the problem on which he has consulted me. As it was his telegram that brought me here, perhaps it should be he who explains matters to you. Please be as thorough as you like, Hendricks," he added, turning to the professor. "It

will help me to hear all the relevant facts stated again."
With these words Holmes steepled his hands, lay back in
his chair and closed his eyes.

Hendricks turned to me. "I must first confess to a
misgiving, Dr Watson. I fear that I may have brought you
here on a wild goose chase. It was largely in jocular spirit
that I communicated with Mr Sherlock Holmes. As he
mentioned, I have for some years had the pleasure of
reading your most interesting accounts of his cases, and
your reports have made me aware that it is neither the
enormity of a crime, nor the exalted standing of those
concerned in it, that are of importance to our friend, but
the intellectual challenge of solving a mystery. Well, sir, a
little matter arose here which I judged to be exactly to our
friend's taste. It is a matter utterly baffling to us here, and
at the same time so trivial that no-one −certainly not the
police force− could be expected to take it seriously. You
will understand, then, that my intention in mentioning it
to Holmes was more to amuse him than seriously to
request his help. You know that we were undergraduate
friends, and perhaps I am guilty of some remnant of
undergraduate humour in approaching so distinguished a
figure with so inconsiderable a matter. In any event, I
now find, somewhat to my discomfiture, that Europe's
greatest consulting detective and his invaluable ally are
here to investigate our little problem.

"Enough of apologies. Let me put the facts before you.
The marine biology department, for which I am
responsible, has a laboratory for its researches. In it we
keep living specimens of marine life; so many, indeed,
that the lab is jocularly known to some as the Aquarium.
To feed our piscivorous specimens we keep a constant
supply of fish in the cold larder. These fish have been

unaccountably disappearing."

The professor paused, and I waited for him to continue.

He coughed apologetically. "That, I am embarrassed to tell you, is the problem in its entirety," he said. "So you see, Doctor, that I was not guilty of exaggertion when I said that the matter was, in itself, of no importance whatever. But I can assure you that I was not exaggerating either in saying that it has been, to us at least, quite inexplicable. We have puzzled and puzzled over it, without making the least headway. The whole situation raises questions none of which we have been able to answer. Questions such as: who would trouble to steal fish that are readily available for a few pence not ten minutes' walk away, in the town market? Or again: who would be able to do so undetected? I could go on."

"I take it that these are just ordinary fish?" I asked.

"Indeed so. We take whatever is readily available from the fishmongers in the covered market: the heads of the choicer fish, perhaps, or whole mackerel when they are cheap and plentiful. I leave the details to my assistant Johns.

"Let me describe the circumstances. I have two colleagues who work with me in the laboratory, Dr Kerr and Mr Collingwood Wynter. There is also the laboratory assistant I mentioned, Arthur Johns. These three are the only ones, besides myself, who have keys to the building. We also have two advanced students who research there regularly, and on occasion we bring undergraduate students to the laboratory.

"The laboratory consists of one main room and two small offices. The main room houses the tanks and the plant."

"The 'plant'?" I interrupted.

"The equipment needed to regulate the tanks. Their temperature, aeration, salinity and so on must be maintained at the correct levels to preserve the life of the specimens.

"In an alcove in this main room is the larder, where we store the food for the specimens. The food is of various types for the various different specimens we keep, but a good deal of it consists of fresh fish from the market, as I have described. We have an arrangement with the market fishmongers.

"About three weeks ago Johns, our assistant, mentioned to me that we seemed to be getting through more fish than formerly, and asked if he should increase the order. I instructed him to do so, which he did, but still the supply was not enough. Yet Johns was most emphatic that he was not feeding the specimens more than formerly. We were mystified, and decided that Johns should henceforth take careful stock of the food, recording the number of fish fed to the specimens each day. This immediately produced the most strange result. On the first night that Johns started to keep these records, there were eight fish lying in the tin when he left the building. The following morning, he came in and found only five. We assumed some mistake on his part, but no; similar results have obtained night after night. Almost every night two or three fish vanish from the tin. We checked, and checked again. Was Johns dishonest or negligent? We asked ourselves. It seemed unlikely, for the man has served us well and faithfully for years, but to be certain, we arranged that on one night Kerr should stand in for Johns, and on another night that Wynter should do likewise. The substitutions made no difference; on the mornings in question, a few fish were, as usual, found to be missing. We have carefully examined all windows and doors for signs of forced entry, and found none.

"So there we are, Dr Watson. We have been entirely unable either to explain this continued theft of fish, or to end it. We are at a loss."

The professor, having laid the facts before me, shrugged his shoulders, and sat back. He turned to Holmes:

"May I ask what you, sir, what you make of this trivial case?"

"I make nothing of it," replied Holmes, leaning back in his chair. "There are as yet too few facts to go on, and I would no more rush to a hypothesis on insufficient data than would you, Professor. I suggest a visit, as early as is convenient, to the scene of these frightful crimes."

The Professor pulled out his watch. "It is scarcely six o'clock. Dinner will be served in Founder's Hall at eight. If we go to the laboratory now, we shall have more than an hour there. Will that suffice?"

A few minutes' walk through quiet, ancient lanes brought us to the laboratory, a tall brick building set back from the road. The Professor found the outer door unlocked. "Ah! I expect Kerr or Wynter is here, working late," he said, as he let in myself and Sherlock Holmes. We all three moved down the vestibule and entered the main chamber. It was filled with perhaps two dozen glass tanks of different sizes, most of them full of water. The floor was wet and covered with duck-boards. A constant humming, gurgling sound filled the air; it was, the Professor explained, the noise of the filtration and temperature control systems. As he was expatiating on the technicalities of salinity pumps, a door at the far end of the room opened and a man emerged. He saw us, hesitated a moment, and then walked briskly up. He was a russet-haired man of middle years, a little below middle height, with something of the terrier about him.

"May I introduce Dr Kerr?" said the Professor. "Kerr, Dr Watson and Mr Holmes." We were standing by the largest of the glass tanks, and as the formalities of introduction were observed, I saw, over the newcomer's shoulder, something strange: a dark shape, about the size of a man, flapped slowly through the tank from one side to the other.

The professor noticed my surprise. "Our latest acquisition!" said he proudly. "The giant soft-shelled turtle. A most fascinating beast; it comes from the China Sea. Feel how warm the water has to be," he said, putting his palm again the glass. "No, don't do that!" he suddenly exclaimed.

I had lifted up the heavy lid of the tank, and was about to dip my fingers into the water.

"Don't be misled by the creature's lazy movements, Dr Watson; it can strike like a cobra. Last term an undergraduate lost half his finger in that way. One of Wynter's undergraduates. You were present at the time, were you not, Kerr?"

"Indeed I was," Kerr answered. "The young fool was teasing the beast, dabbling its food around in the water. It snapped up half his index finger in an instant – nipped off the top two phalanges, clean through the bone."

I was happy enough to leave this treacherous creature and move on to the next tank. "Ah, this one is less dangerous," said the professor. "Less rare too." I peered through the glass, but could see through the murky water no creature of any kind, only a large rock. "It spends most of the day under that hollow rock," explained the professor. "The common octopus; Dr Kerr here is investigating its ability to change colour to match its background, as does a chameleon. Now, these creatures lie more in my sphere of interest," he continued, indicating a table ranged with tiers of small tanks. The tanks all contained a bed of mud or sand above which the water was clear or cloudy, still or bubbling. Various tubes protuded from the lids, and each tank bore a neat but to me incomprehensible label; '*Turkomans Tekke 83 B/C4 (mangrove)*, I read, or '*Merghi Isl. 82 E8 (litoral)*'.

"We have had these shipped from temperate and tropical waters throughout the world," said the professor. "The variety of marine life contained in these small tanks would astonish you, sir. Every month in this laboratory new species, new genera are discovered. The so-called Glass Shrimp here – a creature quite transparent, with all its internal organs and workings clearly visible; the perfect model for our students." As he spoke, the professor unlocked a glass-fronted cabinet and took from it a box. "Or here, for instance, I can show you a remarkable worm, as yet entirely unknown to science."

Holmes must have fallen behind and slipped away surreptitiously, for as the professor was sliding open the lid of the box, we were interrupted by my friend's voice from the other side of the laboratory.

"Where does this door lead?"

"Ah! Mr Sherlock Holmes returns us to the matter in hand. It leads to a small office; allow me to show you." He crossed the laboratory and unlocked the door for Holmes. The detective entered and peered about him, listened attentively, and tapped upon the walls, until, apparently satisfied, he stepped back into the main chamber. "That alcove yonder I take to be the where the fish are kept," he said, and strode over to it.

It was evident that the alcove was indeed used for storage; in it were piled sacks of salt and sand, coils of tubing for the tanks, and the like. This miscellaneous collection included a meat-safe, standing some two feet above the floor, with a perforated door held shut by a simple catch. Holmes opened it, and brought forth what he and I had come to this great and ancient city to investigate: an enamel dish, containing four mackerel in iced water. This was nothing out of the ordinary, our host assured us. Johns, the laboratory assistant, would have left the fish there, as usual, ready for the morning feed, before going home for the evening. Kerr and the professor wondered if perhaps they should have told Johns of Holmes's visit, but Holmes declared himself content that Johns knew nothing of it, for he wanted no special preparations; wishing, on the contrary, to find everything on his visit as it would have been at any other time. As he spoke, Holmes was inspecting the alcove with his customary care, examining with particular attention the ventilation bricks behind the meat-safe. This done, he asked to be shown the remaining rooms that comprised the Marine Department of the School. These were two small offices, one each for Professor Hendricks and Dr Kerr, accessible from the main chamber where we stood. Mr Wynter had his office on the other side of the vestibule, on the part of the building given over to the rest of the School of Natural History. The three offices were examined in turn by Holmes, tapping here and there on the walls, and peering at the floor and desk tops and window-ledges through his magnifying lens.

At length his investigation of the premises was completed. The two dons were naurally eager to know if he had come to any conclusion, but he would not be drawn. "I have seen all I can usefully see here, gentlemen. Dinner is at eight o'clock, I believe you said. I shall spend the time until then considering this interesting little problem.

"One last question, Professor: do you know where your colleague Mr Wynter is to be found?"

"Good Lord, you don't suspect Wynter, do you?" asked the professor with a nervous laugh. But still Holmes would not be drawn. "I suspect everybody," he replied with a bland smile. "It is my *métier*."

"I cannot tell you with any certainty where he is to be found at this moment. Do you know, Kerr?"

"I do not,' said he, 'but he told me that he is intending to dine in Hall tonight."

"Excellent!" cried Holmes. "I wish you a pleasant evening, gentlemen. Until eight o'clock!" And with these words he turned on his heel and left us.

The remaining three of us went our separate ways. I made a solitary return to All Saints through the University Gardens, which now, as the sun was setting, were almost deserted of visitors. The path of the river guided me back by a meandering route to the college. There I found Professor Hendricks and Dr Kerr in the company of a third man, gaunt and stiff, who was introduced to me as Mr Collingwood Wynter. He, I remembered, was the man who had sat up alone in the laboratory all one night, in an attempt to surprise the thief. We had not sat talking long before Holmes joined us, completing our little party. He begged leave to ask a few questions of Wynter: where exactly he had passed that night when he had waited up for the intruder or intruders, and what he had heard and seen? Wynter's answer was that he had passed the night in the vestibule, and had seen and heard nothing. He himself had himself thoroughly checked the offices and other rooms, and locked them. No entry into the main laboratory was possible except by way of the vestibule, in which he had sat awake all night, fortified by black coffee. These answers seemed to satisfy Holmes, and our conversation became general. At eight o'clock the bell sounded, and all in the common-room, guests and dons alike, rose and followed the master into the hall. Dinner was served to us at the head of the hall, while below us sat the undergraduates, a livelier and noisier company than their elders.

We five were a little constrained. There was some suppressed excitement, as we wondered if the secret of the laboratory fish was soon to be revealed, mingled perhaps with some mutual suspicion between the three colleagues. Talk did not flow freely; topics of conversation were pursued with the simulated enthusiasm of those who are determined to talk of anything other than what is uppermost in their thoughts. It was not until dessert was over and the port circulating that Kerr finally broke the ice, by asking Holmes outright if he had found a solution to the mystery. The answer, given as casually as if he were giving us the time of day, was that he had. He had identified the thief, and it only remained to confirm the identification by observation. The thief would almost certainly steal that night, as was his habit, and any of us who cared to join Holmes in a night vigil at the laboratory would be able to witness the theft. We pressed Holmes to identify the culprit, but he refused to do so. "Come, gentlemen, I have hidden nothing from you; you have the same evidence to guide you as I do. Does the solution not suggest itself to any of you?" He looked to us each in turn, but no answer was forthcoming. The hint of a smile flickered across his lean face. "No matter. In a few hours you shall see for yourselves. Still, it might amuse you in the meantime to see if deduction will enable you to predict what we will see. I would advise you to consider two matters. First, the matter of motive. Who has something to gain by removing the fish? Why would that individual not go to the fishmonger's? The second matter is that of means. Who could have gained access to the fish? Mr Wynter told us that on the night of his vigil all means of entry were secure, and anyone entering the laboratory must have first passed him. He says nobody passed him. What do you conclude from that?" With these remarks, Holmes left us to our own devices, and would answer no further questions on the topic.

At eleven o'clock that night we left the college and followed the mediaeval alleys leading to the 'aquarium'. As Hendricks was unlocking the outer door, Holmes earnestly enjoined us to complete silence from the moment that we were in the building, and insisted too that no lights be lit, with the result that, once in the building, we were obliged to grope our way to our place of concealment. This, Holmes had decided, was to be Dr Kerr's office, whose windows gave a view of the main laboratory, including the alcove containing the fish. We settled down in the dark and waited. At first the laboratory seemed as black as pitch, but as my eyes adjusted I was able to make out a few details that detached themselves from the general darkness: a gleam from some pail or carboy, the doors to the other parts of the building, the skylight glimmering overhead, and the huge tanks. Once I made out the silhouette I had seen earlier of the giant turtle swimming silently in its tank.

The minutes crawled by; a few whispered words from Kerr were peremptorily hushed by Holmes, and thereafter we all remained quite still and silent. As I looked at the doors and the skylight I wondered where the intruder would make his entrance. Holmes evidently did not expect any danger, for he had asked me to leave my revolver in my room. It was a long night. The hours of our vigil were marked by the bells of the city, some chiming the quarter hours, and all, far and near, sounding the hours. Midnight passed, and one o'clock; it was shortly after a quarter past one when a sound came from within the laboratory. It was a subdued, rasping sound. We all held our breath. I looked up at the skylight, but saw nothing there moving. Something seemed to be shifting in the darkness of the empty laboratory; the lid of one of the tanks was rising a few inches, then moving slowly forward. When it had inched forward by a third of its length, it stopped moving, and what seemed to be two tapering snakes emerged, then a third, and a fourth, followed by a bulky form easing itself out. The octopus was crawling out of its tank. It slithered down the glass to the slatted floor, and walked over to the meat-safe. With a tentacle it lifted the latch, opened the door and reached inside, whence it brought out a mackerel. With another tentacle it pulled the head off and fed it into its mouth. For a few moments the creature stood there eating, the leathery skin around its beak moving as it chewed. Its eye, slotted like a goat's, swivelled as it ate, but we, heedful of its surveillance, remained perfectly still, our breath bated, and the beast, unaware that it was under observation, continued its meal. With the now headless fish held in one tentacle, another reached out into the safe and withdrew holding a second fish, whereupon a third tentacle daintily closed the safe door. The creature turned and walked back to the tank, carrying the two fish, and slithered up the glass wall as easily as it had come down. Carefully it squeezed itself under the lid into the tank and lowered itself into the water. I heard a whispered 'Good Lord!' beside me as several tentacles reached up to manoeuvre the lid of the tank back into place. Safely covered again, the beast sank down through the water to the bottom of the tank, where it crept in under its rock out of sight, no doubt to consume its haul in secrecy.

We exchanged glances of astonishment and disbelief at what we had witnessed. It was indeed one of the most extraordinary sights I have ever seen, and not the least extraordinary thing about it was that not a sign was now to be seen of what had occurred, for the scene before our eyes was in every way identical to that which had confronted us at the beginning of our sojourn. The tanks stood dark in the moonlight, all securely lidded, as before. Any watery tracks left by the octopus had already merged indistinguishably with the constant dampness of the floor. Across from the tanks we could see the door to the safe, carefully closed, just as Johns had left it. It was as if we had fallen asleep, and the weird beast had emerged from our dreams, or nightmares. The only sign that we had not been dreaming was out of sight behind the safe door: two missing fish.

"Of course, one can hardly suppose that the beast replaced the lid of its tank in order deliberately to erase any evidence of its excursion," explained Dr Kerr. We were walking back to the College in the moonlight, our footfalls echoing in the empty lanes. "Foresight of that kind cannot properly be ascribed to the lower creation," he continued, emphasing his remarks with abrupt gestures of the hand as if he were in the lecture hall. "But there is no doubt that the common octopus is a creature both intelligent and secretive. In the wild it lurks in small caves and under rocks, and will go to great lengths to hide its presence. There are numerous instances of it rolling stones before the entrance to its cave, so that it may remain undetected. The creature seems to have an instinct for deception and concealment, for covering its tracks. I suggest that in replacing the tank lid, it was merely following as nearly as it might the promptings of its nature, the tank taking the place of the kind of rock cavity where the common octopus is usually to be found."

"Yes, I'm sure you're right, Kerr," interposed the professor. "Tell me, Mr Holmes, were you as surprised as we were, or did you already suspect our octopedal thief?"

"I did indeed have some suspicions, professor, although I'm sure that the sight of the octopus carrying out his work astonished me no less than it did you. You have read Watson's accounts of my cases; perhaps you recall a maxim of mine, that once all other possibilities have been eliminated, that which remains, however improbable, must be true. That principle I applied in this instance. It was obvious from the sojourns in the hallway that the culprit could not have entered unobserved from outside; one sentinel on one occasion might have nodded, but not Kerr, Johns and you, on each of several separate occasions. My thorough examination of the laboratory and its adjoining rooms confirmed that no forcible entry or intrusion had been made. Therefore, the disappearance of the fish was effected somehow from within the laboratory. How that might be possible, I could not guess, so I then turned my attention to another matter, that of motive. I asked myself two questions: who would so desire a few mackerel as to steal and risk discovery, and why would he not buy them from the fishmonger's? The questions were decisive. I should be ashamed to tell you for how long I puzzled over them, but eventually the only possible answer came to me."

"We are all grateful to you for solving our little problem, Mr Holmes," said Hendricks, "but I must apologise for having involved you in a matter so far beneath –"

"My dear Hendricks," interrupted Holmes, clapping his friend upon the shoulder, "no apology is necessary, I assure you. I appreciate a worthy opponent, and your octopus is certainly one of the most gifted and accomplished thieves I have ever known. To watch him at his work has been a privilege."

The Case of
the Apprentice's Notebook

IT WAS A DARK NOVEMBER afternoon, and I was making my way to the Baker Street rooms I shared with Mr Sherlock Holmes. As I huddled in my cab, icy blasts of rain came lashing through the window, and I was delighted to discover upon entering the flat that Mrs Hudson had already lit a fire. I was even more delighted when she brought up a tray of muffins and tea. Holmes was not at home, and while Mrs Hudson bustled about laying the table, I asked her if she expected his early return.

"Do you suppose I can tell you?" the long-suffering landlady replied. "All these years Mr Holmes has been with me, and I'm blest if I've once known when he'll be back. It might be five minutes, or it might be five weeks. With some of these cases he gets himself involved in, it's a wonder he comes back at all. What I can tell you, though," she added, "is that he had two visitors this morning, just after you left. But where he went, or when he'll be back, that I truly couldn't tell you."

"Two visitors, you say?"

"Two women, sir. One young one, and the other older,

as who might have been her mother."

"And he left with them, you say?"

"No, sir. After a while the two of them came downstairs and left together, and then half-an-hour later Mr Holmes left. Will that be all?"

"Thank you, Mrs Hudson."

I ate my tea alone, and then settled myself by the fire to read the newspaper in comfort. The heat of the fire made me drowsy as I read, and I was drifting off into slumber when the sudden slamming of the street door startled me awake. Footsteps came bounding up the stairs, and in burst Holmes, damp and ruddy-faced. He flung his cape and deer-stalker in a wet heap on the sofa, and sank into his armchair. For a few moments he stretched himself before the fire, saying nothing. The niceities of social intercourse were ever a matter of indifference to him.

"A profitable day, Holmes?" I ventured.

"Not entirely. Nor for you, I fancy. I see your patient died this morning."

"How on earth did you know that?"

"The signs are obvious enough," he replied with a shrug.

"Not to me. You would do me a very great favour if you told me what they are, so that I might hide them. The death of a patient is hardly something one likes to proclaim to the world."

Holmes leaned back in his chair, drew on his pipe, and closed his eyes.

"They will be easy enough to expunge, Watson. A pumice-stone and soap-and-water will suffice. Glance at the fingers of your right hand."

"Ah! Ink-stains. I thought I had washed them off. Still,

I fail to see why they proclaim the death of my patient."

"Most of the ink you did wash off, but some stubbornly remains, as you see, in a little channel on the second forefinger of your right hand. That of course is where the pen rests when you write, and it requires a good many hours of writing to press that groove into the finger and engrain it with ink. Evidently, then, you spent most of the day writing. However, you had told me this morning that you were at present involved in a very difficult case; your patient's life was in the balance, you said, and, expecting to be tending him all day, you had arranged for a colleague to undertake the care of your other patients. Now," continued Holmes, "you had gone to some trouble to reserve the whole day for the care of your patient, and yet you spent it writing. What can that mean, but the death of the patient?

"Those ink-stains tell me more," he continued. "You use black Chinese ink for your medical records, whereas the blue-black ink whose traces remain on your hand is the ink you use for correspondence, and for recording the detection cases in which you are kind enough to help me. You would hardly have spent all day on your private correspondence, I think. So," he said, pointing at me a long, bony, admonitory finger, "I conclude that you have spent most of the day writing up some new case to inflict on your public. Come now, Watson, confess that you have been found out. What instance of the science of detection you have been embroidering this time with the gaudy colours of adventure and romance?"

"You shall know that when it is finished. I am pleased that I still have one or two secrets hidden from your analytic gaze."

Holmes smiled, and said no more, merely gazing into

the fire as the wreaths of smoke that rose from his pipe gradually filled the room. I was waiting for him to tell me something of his visitors earlier in the day, but he was not forthcoming.

Eventually my curiosity became too much for me. "Mrs Hudson tells me you had visitors this morning," I said.

"So I did," he replied, throwing a fresh log onto the fire, and sending a shower of sparks up the chimney. He leaned back again in his chair and sighed. "Alas, Watson, I seem to have come down in the world since the summer, when I was advising half the governments and royal houses of Europe. My visitors today were Mrs Mary Garrity and Miss Nelly Moore, of Walworth, who sought my advice about the disappearance of Mrs Garrity's son, a builder's apprentice."

I was not pleased to hear that Holmes was already interesting himself in a new case, however humble, before he was fully recovered from his excessive efforts earlier in the year. Once decided to act, he would spare no efforts, and would trace a builder's apprentice as tirelessly as he would the son of a Duke. Yet I fought back my impulse to advise him against taking on the case, for I knew that once his mind was made up, nothing I could say would dissuade him; one might as well whistle back the greyhound that has sighted a hare. I was resigned to hearing the worst when I asked Holmes if he would be taking up the case.

"I have decided to look into it, yes. And you need not trouble to express your disapproval, old fellow. Your face is as an open book. Would you nevertheless like me to rehearse the few facts I have been able to ascertain?"

"I should be most interested to hear about it, Holmes."

"Then you shall. Mrs Garrity, my visitor this morning,

is a widow, and the mother of one son, James, a lad of seventeen years. Nelly Moore, the other visitor, is a particular friend of James – his sweetheart, I should say. Some twenty years ago Mrs Garrity, newly married, came with her husband to England, and settled in London. Her husband was more of a drinker than a worker, it seems. He died when James was five years old, leaving Mrs Garrity alone to fend for herself and her infant son. She found work in the steam-laundry in Brixton, where she works to this day. She and her son live in Walworth. Early this year young James was apprenticed to a local builder. The firm is a thriving one, and the position offered a fair future to the lad. All seemed well until three weeks ago, when James failed to come home from work. He has not been seen since. Such behaviour is entirely out of character, they assure me, and neither mother nor sweetheart can think of any reason for his sudden disappearance. The constabulary has not been able to help, and as a last resort they came to me.

"As you know, I am not presently engaged in any case, and I took up the matter immediately. Don't shake your head in that disapproving way, Watson. I appreciate that you are concerned lest I overtax myself, but I think you will admit in the first place that I have a pretty strong constitution, and in the second that to a nature such as mine idleness is a greater evil than overwork. As I say, I accepted the case, and my first point of enquiry was the boy's apprentice-master. The man's name is Seth Armstrong. He has his builder's yard and office in Camberwell, at a short walk from the Garritys' rooms in Walworth. I went there this morning, after my visitors had left, but I found that Armstrong was in Bromley, where he had a job in hand. To Bromley I went, and spoke first to the labourers on the site. They remembered Garrity well, and with some affection, but they were not as a group quite unanimous about when he was last seen. All were sure that he was at the previous job, in Hampshire, which had finished three weeks earlier, but whereas some seemed to think he had been at the present site of work, if only for a few days, others could not remember seeing him there at all. I then introduced myself to Armstrong, a tall, strong man in early middle age; a confident, affable kind of fellow. He was able to give me more definite information about the boy than had his men: Garrity had indeed been present at Bromley for the first day, he told me, but had not presented himself for work again. The date of the boy's disappearance may well be of some importance, of course, so I asked to see the firm's time-sheet records. They confirmed what Armstrong had told me.

"Armstrong said that he had taken on young Garrity as an apprentice builder, but in fact the boy's work was more that of an apprentice works surveyor."

"A 'works surveyor'?" I queried.

"Ah, there I have the advantage of you, Watson, having spent the day amongst the building trade. A works' surveyor checks on quantities and types of materials used, when and where the materials were delivered, and at what cost, how much returned to suppliers, and so on. Such were Garrity's duties, and in this matter at least the master's word was corroborated by his men, who had told me that it was something of a standing joke among them, that Garrity might turn up anywhere with his notebook, and start jotting down notes upon the size and provenance of some pile of sand or bag of nails.

"I told Armstrong that I would like to see this notebook, whereupon he replied with a sudden oath that he would like to see it himself, and roundly cursed the boy for having run off with it.

"And that, Watson, is all I could find out today. Try as I might, I could establish no more than the background picture I have just given you. A poor day's work for England's foremost consulting detective," he said with a bitter smile. "Lestrade would have done as much."

Holmes, who had been filling his favourite meerschaum as he spoke, now seized a live coal in the fire-tongs and lit his pipe at it. "So there you are," he said between puffs. "Well, perhaps tomorrow will bring more. Where do I start? That is my problem. It seems an ordinary case of a missing person, and it is always these ordinary cases that are the most difficult. A *point d'entrée,* Watson, that is what these commonplace cases lack, some oddity, some little anomaly on the surface that will lead to the rotten core. Without such a clue I am unable –"

Holmes stopped in mid-sentence.

"The front door! Who can it be at this hour?'

Mrs Hudson opened the door and announced: "Mrs Garrity."

A small, sharp-faced woman of some forty years took a few steps into the room. Her face, that had once been handsome, was care-worn and lined, and her hair was silver. She bore every sign of agitation in her manner, and the poor woman was dripped with rain as she stood before us.

"Come in, Mrs Garrity!" said Holmes. "You may lay your coat before the fire. What brings you across London in this weather?"

"He's been back, sir, he's been back!" she cried,

clasping and unclasping her hands before her in her excitement.

"This is excellent news," replied Holmes, "after these three weeks. My felicitations! James is well, I hope?"

The question gave our visitor pause, and a shadow passed over her face. "That I cannot say, for I never saw him. Back, and straightway gone away again!" She looked from one of us to the other, wringing her hands.

"You are naturally upset, Mrs Garrity," said Holmes. "Pray sit by the fire here, and compose yourself. I shall fetch you a glass of port-wine. When you are settled, you will tell me and Dr Watson what has happened."

"Thank you, sir."

"I have been looking into your case today," said Holmes as he unstopped the decanter, "and I am sorry to say that I have so far made little headway. It seems that you know more of the recent whereabouts of your son than I," he continued, handing her the glass. "Are you ready to tell us what happened today? You may speak quite freely before Dr Watson."

She sipped her wine, put down the glass, and began her narrative:

"It was when I got back from the steam-laundry this afternoon. I was working an early shift, and arrived home just after four o'clock. I went to unlock the door as usual, but it wouldn't unlock, as it was already unlocked, do you see, and just pulled to."

"One moment, if you please," interrupted Holmes. "Do you say that it was unusual for the door to be left unlocked?"

"Oh, indeed. We always keep the door locked."

"Proceed."

"The moment I went in, I knew right away someone

had been there before me. I've never seen the place like it. There were things lying all over, most of all in James's room. Then in the kitchen I found this note from James. I brought it to show you, Mr Holmes. Here it is." Mrs Garrity handed over a torn sheet of paper:

HAVE MOVED AWAY. ALL IS WELL
 DO NOT WORRY
J

Holmes looked at it carefuly, frowning. "I should like to keep this for the present. Is this your son's hand?"

The question brought a look of puzzlement to Mrs Garrity's face. "I have been asking myself the self-same question, Mr Holmes. It is hard to say, it being in great letters. Sometimes I think it is, but then sometimes again I think not."

"I suppose you have no other example of his handwriting here?"

"I have not, sir. I'm sorry for that. Do you think he did not write it himself?"

"That I cannot say. Will you tell us more about the state in which you found your rooms?"

"What can I tell you? But that they were all awry, things pulled onto the floor and scattered abroad. Poor James, he must have been in a dreadful hurry to have left our home like that. He's a neat boy, you understand, always tidy. I've never known him to leave his room in such a state."

"Did you notice if anything was missing?"

"I did not, sir, no."

"And did you tidy your rooms before you came here

tonight?"

"No, I came here straight away, Mr Holmes."

"Excellent! You did well to come here and tell me of this, Mrs Garrity, and to leave your rooms as you found them. I want you to leave them untouched tonight also. I shall come round to you in the morning, and see them for myself. In the meantime, I suggest you take another glass of port-wine. It is a cold, wet night."

But Mrs Garrity refused, saying she must get back to Walworth. We could hear the rain falling outside, and the wind gusting. My friend gave Mrs Garrity a sovereign for a cab to take her home. That too she refused at first, but in the end Holmes prevailed upon her, and away she went into the night.

We returned to our seats by the fire. "Poor creature!" I said. "She hardly seemed to know what to make of her son's return. Is he her only son?"

"He is. Well, Watson, It seems I am for Walworth tomorrow."

"Would my presence be of any help? I should be pleased to accompany you."

"That is what I hoped to hear, Watson. Your presence would be of the greatest help to me."

"Then of course I shall come. I do not look forward with enthusiasm to another day cooped up in my consulting-room."

"Good man! We shall go down to Walworth first thing in the morning."

The sky had cleared, and the sun was shining on the wet pavements of Walworth, as Holmes and I made our way to Mrs Garrity's. We had turned off the main road into a tangle of narrow streets, and threading our way through them we finally came to the address we were seeking. The street door was opened to us by Mrs Garrity herself. She led us up a flight of stairs to a dark landing smelling of onions, opened her appartment door, and led us in.

We found ourselves in a narrow corridor, with four rooms leading off it, two on each side. The floors were of wooden boards, with rush matting laid over them in the parlour. Holmes, with his usual disregard for social pleasanteries, sprang into action immediately. He had Mrs Garrity light the gas in the passage and knelt down to examine the boards with his magnifying lens. Like a dog following a scent, he moved back and forth across the hall, and in and out the rooms, following, it seemed, some invisible track that led him all over the little flat. Twice he took from his pocket a tape-measure and measured some mark or object on the floor too small for me to see, and once he scraped up with his knife something which he put carefully into a fold of paper and into his pocket. When he had finished his examination of the floor he sprang to his feet and asked Mrs Garrity about the disruption to the rooms. It was her son's room that had been disturbed most, she said, as if he had been looking for something of his – perhaps clothes. While she was talking, Holmes moved into James's room, Mrs Garrity and I following him. He fell to examining the chest of drawers, trying how the drawers ran in their grooves. Some seemed to be wedged tight, but moved smoothly once Holmes had carefully unjammed them. Noticing his efforts, Mrs Garrity explained that her son would regularly wax the drawers with candle-ends until they ran easy. Holmes nodded absently, as if little interested in her remarks, and then knelt down to look under the bed. He would be lucky to find anything there, Mrs Garrity warned him, as her son never kept anything under the bed, and she was proved right. Clothes and a pair of the lad's shoes were next to be inspected. That done, Holmes turned his attention to a notebook of the boy's that had been in one of the drawers. He took it over to the window and, producing from his breast-pocket the note Mrs Garrity had left at Baker Street the previous evening, compared the two, holding them this way and that, at different angles to the light, peering from one to the other through his magnifier. At last he was satisfied that he had seen all he could. Pocketing his glass and the papers, he turned from the window and thanked Mrs Garrity for her trouble. She was so delighted her son had returned, she told us, but her delight was of course spoiled by her having missed seeing him. She believed and hoped fervently that she would see him soon. Holmes's response was honest, even to the point of harshness: "I hope so, too, but these, I fear, are murky waters, too murky to see what lies ahead. Still, I have reason to believe we shall shortly know what has become of your son. You may expect some news soon, Mrs Garrity. Goodbye."

We left her standing forlorn in her doorway, and made our way down the stairs into the street.

"Of course, it was not James Garrity who entered that apartment yesterday." Holmes was expatiating on the case as we walked briskly through the back streets of Walworth. "It is fortunate that yesterday was a wet day. Muddy prints had been left on the floor, faint, but visible. Whoever left them wore boots four sizes larger than Garrity's. And did you notice the jammed drawers,

Watson? They were jammed because they had been thrust violently back at an angle. Was it Garrity who slammed them back so clumsily, the neat young fellow who had waxed them until they glided in and out? I think not."

Our way –the same way we had come – led us through a narrow defile into the Walworth Road, a broad highway where the street-traffic, human and equine, rushed along in a torrent.

"And what of the note?" I asked him. "Was that written by the young man?"

"Ah yes, the note. The note is interesting – a most suggestive piece of evidence. In form, its letters resemble those of Garrity's hand as I saw it in his notebook. But they had been uncertainly made, with wavering strokes and one or two corrections. And the pressure was heavier than in the notebooks; quite a furrow had been dug into the paper with the pencil. Yet the table-top on which the note was found, a top of soft deal, showed no sign of bruising from a pencil, nor did any other likely surface. The pencil itself, by the way, was a carpenter's pencil, as was apparent from the varying thickness of the line according to the angle of the stroke."

"Perhaps I am being unusually slow, Holmes, but I can't see what that tells us about the matter."

"It tells us that the note was probably written elsewhere, earlier, and – "

"I still don't see how it tells us that."

"On what surface did he rest the paper to write?" he answered impatiently. "On nothing in the apartment, or some scoring would have marked it. Therefore, it was written elsewhere. Why? So that the writer could practise copying Garrity's hand, I suggest. That hypothesis is borne out by the hesitant nature of the strokes and the number of careful little corrections."

"But the front door, Holmes. It had not been forced; it had been unlocked. How to explain that, unless it was the son who unlocked it? Who else had a key?"

"Bravo, Watson! A most pertinent question. I suspect that the answer to it lies in the village of Great Mowl. That way lies Waterloo Station," he said, pointing. "Are you still ready for the chase?"

"Of course, Holmes. But Great Mowl? I've never heard of the place. Where is it? And what has it to do with James Garrity?"

"It lies at the western end of the North Downs. Your other question I shall answer once we are on the train," he replied, increasing his pace.

The train was not long to wait, and when we were seated Holmes was as good as his word. "As you are good enough to accompany me to Great Mowl, Watson, I owe you an explanation of our journey. I told you of my visit to see Armstrong and his men at Bromley yesterday, did I not? You will remember that there was some discrepancy between what the labourers told me about where Garrity was last seen, and what Armstrong told me. Armstrong was positive that young Garrity had been at Bromley for the first two days of the job, and then vanished. But Garrity's workmates were a good deal less definite about it: not one of them could swear to having seen him on the Bromley site. They well remembered having seen him at the previous job, however. That job was at the vicarage of Great Mowl. So Great Mowl is now left as the last place where we know the lad was seen. What we will find there, I do not know, but it is where the scent leads, and we must follow."

"And now, my dear fellow, I shall take a catnap. A busy day lies ahead of us, and we must be ready for whatever it may bring." So saying he gathered his greatcoat around him and fell asleep, while the train, having left behind the suburbs of London, carried us through the fields and copses of Surrey.

We were the only passengers to alight at the little railway station of Great Mowl. How different it was, that quiet place, from the narrow back-streets of Walworth. The station was a mile from the village, and as we made our way to the vicarage we seemed to have gone back to another, older world; the unchanging world of old England, with its elms, its ancient church, its quiet fields and hedgerows. Whatever upheavals might threaten in the great world, whatever wars and empires might be won and lost, while these villages remain, England must remain too, for they are its heart. It was strange to think that our search for the dark, perhaps criminal secret behind the disappearance of young James Garrity should lead us to such a place. The lane from the station took us past fields at first, then a shop, a public-house, and a row of cottages, before bringing us to the village green, where our arrival was noisily greeted by the ducks on the pond. On one side of us stood the church, and on the other the gates of the vicarage. We walked through the gates and up a mossy drive, the trees on either side of us still dripping from last night's rain. A house-keeper answered our knock at the door and admitted us into a small hall, where Holmes handed her his card to be presented to the vicar. We had but a few seconds to wait before she returned to usher us into the study, where a fire was already burning. The tall, willowy figure of the Reverend

Nathaniel Flowerdew rose from behind his desk to greet us. "I am delighted to meet you, Mr Sherlock Holmes," he enthused, beaming behind his spectacles and bowing. "Pray take a seat."

"I hope we do not interrupt you."

"Not in the least, my dear sirs, not in the least! I was merely scribbling a few stray thoughts upon Theocritus." He closed the volume before him on the desk, wiped his nib and tidied together some stray papers. "Now, gentlemen, how may I help you?"

"I am, as my card has told you, a private consulting detective, and this is my friend and colleague Dr Watson. I am presently engaged to look into the disappearance of one James Garrity. I believe he was involved in recent building work here in your vicarage as an apprentice."

"That is quite possible," answered the vicar. "We have recently been visited by a tribe of builders, of which he may well have been a member. They were engaged in building a conservatory on to the back of the house, a heated conservatory. It had long been a dream of mine, gentlemen. The conservatory is constructed according to a design of my own, based upon the Moorish pleasure gardens of Granada. Perhaps it would interest you to see it?"

"It would interest me very much," answered Holmes, somewhat to my surprise. Flowerdew escorted us out of the study and down the hall to the back of the house. Passing through what had obviously been until recently the back door, we seemed to have been transported to the gardens at Kew. Under an elaborate iron-and-glass roof, we admired in succession, as the vicar brought them to our attention, Moorish spandrels, monstrous plants from the jungles of Burma or Peru, and an elaborate system of water-pipes designed to both hydrate and heat the whole. Holmes examined the work with apparent enthusiasm. He evinced an especial interest in the plumbing work, and followed the hot-water pipes where they ran round the low retaining wall upon which the glass-and-iron work of the conservatory rested. They led us down to a cellar, which, as we discovered, housed the furnace that heated them. Returning at last to ground level, we dutifully expressed, to Flowerdew's delight, our admiration for his new conservatory.

"Were there any other building works carried out?" asked Holmes.

"This was the principal work, of course, but I also had the stable extended, and some repairs made to the kitchen garden wall. Would you wish to see the work?"

"If you have no objection. But do not trouble yourself unnecessarily, I beg you. We will escort ourselves."

The reverend Flowerdew beamed, and rang the bell. "My housekeeper will show you round, gentlemen. Mrs Stamp, would you be good enough to show these gentlemen whatever they wish to see?"

"This way, if you please," she said, and led us out of the conservatory into the garden. Holmes asked her what she could tell us of young Garrity, but what she could tell us was little enough. Garrity, like many of the others, had been present on some days and not on others. When he was there, he was often to be seen with a note-book, counting bricks, sacks, lengths of timber, sheets of glass, and such materials, and jotting down the figures in his book. On the subject of Mr Armstrong she was more eloquent, stressing in particular his defects. Of these he had many, if Mrs Stamp was to be believed, the worst being the habit of constantly carrying a bag of shrimps from which he ate, leaving behind him wherever he went a trail of shrimps' heads, without regard for those who might have to clean up behind him.

When we came to the kitchen garden, we found Mr Stamp, a stocky, red-faced man, digging over a muddy vegetable patch. At our arrival he looked up and stopped digging. The rain was starting to fall again, and all four of us adjourned to a nearby potting-shed. It was windowless and gave off a dusty, doggy smell, but it was dry. Stamp, in the earthy comfort of the shed, told us what he could about Armstrong and his team of builders. He shared his wife's low opinion of them. Their language had been full of profanity, he told us, and their behaviour sinful; they were given to taking strong liquor and playing at cards. This sinfulness, and the wickedness of building exotic glass palaces, not natural in this country, had not gone unpunished. The day that the work had finished, a Chinese vase that had stood for years on the drawing-room mantelpiece fell when no-one was in the room and smashed to smithereens in the fire-place. At about the same time a ghost began to visit the cellar where the furnace was. Muffled groans and howls had been heard, and knockings in the night, and other such unearthly noises. Holmes and I wondered if we might be able to hear the ghost for ourselves, but it seemed we were too late; after a fortnight or so, the visitations had faded away. The presence of evil spirits seemed to be an *idée fixe* of the Stamps, for when the shower of rain passed, allowing us to emerge from our cramped shelter and move on to the stables, we were informed that there too the building work had raised malign spirits. They had entered the mare, to make her ill-tempered and unnaturally restless at night.

Holmes thanked the Stamps for their help, and they left us. He had borne their tales of the supernatural with great patience, and in this I had thought it best to follow his example, but I was not displeased when the stories came to an end and our search for the apprentice could continue in earnest. Holmes did not return immediately to the house, but stood for a while in the stable yard, as still as a statue, staring unseeing into the distance as he pondered the problem in hand. Soon his calculations were done, for all at once he sprang into action, peering with the greatest intensity at the brickwork, new and old, of the stable wall. That done, he strode on to the conservatory, and went straightway went down to the cellar, leaving me above. There being nothing I could do to help him at this point, I thought it better to let him alone in his work. I heard his steps as he scurried about below me, scraping and tapping. Eventually he surfaced, and we rejoined the Reverend Flowerdew in his study where Mrs Stamp had prepared coffee for Holmes and me. The vicar himself took an infusion of Earl Grey's tea, as being less stimulating to the nerves. He was able to confirm what the Stamps had told us about the external building works done by Armstrong, but was less willing to confirm their tales of evil spirits. Though a reliable and god-fearing couple, they were excessively superstitious, he told us, much given to interpreting biblical references to the spirit in too narrowly literal a sense. As he pointed out, strange noises and unease in the horses were to be expected during building works, and scarcely required the spirit world as explanation. In any event, the Stamps' quarters were in the back part of the house, next to the kitchen and scullery, so it was they who had been closest to the noise and disruption. "I am sorry to be so little help in these ghostly matters," he smiled in apology. "Are your enquiries are bearing fruit elsewhere? Have you located the young person?"

"I think I know where he is, Mr Flowerdew."

The vicar looked at Holmes aghast. He was clearly shaken by my friend's reply, and indeed I was astonished by it myself. Holmes had said nothing to me to indicate that he had the least idea where Garrity might be found.

"I think I know, but I am not yet certain," he continued. "A few questions to the Stamps will confirm or deny my suspicions. Would you be good enough to call them?"

Flowerdew rang the bell. We all waited. The room seemed very quiet; one could hear every crackle of the fire. It was a long, awkward wait, and I for one was relieved when Mrs Stamp came in. Flowerdew cleared his throat. "Mr Holmes would like a few words with you and Stamp," he said. "Where is your husband?"

"He's just taking his dinner, sir. Will I fetch him?"

"If you please."

She went out, and reappeared with her husband. They stood before us.

"You told me just now that you thought your quarters were haunted," said Holmes. At his words the Stamps looked uncomfortable, Mrs Stamp glancing at the vicar, and Stamp looking down at his boots while he chewed the remains of his dinner.

"Please tell me again, if you would, what signs of haunting you noticed."

It was Stamp who replied. "We heard groaning, sir, as from a distance, muffled — "

"Where were you when you heard these sounds?" interrupted Holmes.

"It was in our own quarters."

"Always there? Nowhere else?"

"I do believe so, yes," answered Stamp sheepishly, while Flowerdew favoured me with a secret smile, as if to say, "Notice that the haunting was audible only to the gullible."

" 'Groaning' ", repeated Holmes. "What other sounds did you hear?"

"There was a hollow metallic striking noise, and – well, sir, it's hard to say, whispery scraping noises, sometimes, and at other times a kind of far away thumping." Mrs Stamp leaned towards her husband and whispered in his ear.

"There may also have been a kind of howling, or inhuman shouting," he added. "Or then again, it may have been a fox in the night."

"Where did these sounds originate?"

"They came up from the bowels of the earth."

"Thank you. And can you and your wife remember when these noises started?"

"When the man Armstrong and his men up and left, that very night."

"Remarkable! And when was it quiet again?"

"Well, there, it is not so easy to say, exactly, as it faded away, as you might say, over two or three days. In all it was perhaps a week before the spirits quietened down, and left us."

Holmes turned to Flowerdew. "I believe you heard nothing of all this?"

"That is correct, Mr Holmes," came the answer.

Holmes nodded to the priest and turned again to the Stamps: "Thank you. Your answers have been very helpful. Tell me, Stamp, have you a sledgehammer?

Good. Please fetch it, and bring a lantern too."

When the pair had left the room, Holmes spoke in a sombre tone. "Mr Flowerdew, I am very close to the end of my enquiry. In order to confirm my suspicions, and reveal the truth, I must ask you to allow a part of your property to be destroyed. The damage will be small – a matter of a few bricks – and readily repaired. Do we have your permission? May we settle this question once and for all?"

The vicar blanched at this sinister turn of events, but offered no objection. "Of course, Mr Holmes, if you consider it necessary," he answered in a wavering voice. "I would not wish to stand in your way." At this point Stamp returned, carrying lantern and hammer, and stationed himself by the door awaiting orders.

"I fear that the object of my search lies in the cellar, behind the furnace," announced Holmes. "I suggest we go down."

And so we did, in solemn procession; Holmes, Flowerdew (holding a handkerchief to his face), myself (holding the lantern), and, stumping along behind us, a fearsome hammer over his shoulder, Stamp. We descended the little stairway, all of us but Stamp ducking our heads to avoid the roof. It was a tiny cellar, some two yards high, two yards across and perhaps three deep. We were cramped in the little space, and the poor vicar was obliged to stoop lest he strike his head against the ceiling. He made a most unhappy figure, hunched up, his shadow from the lamp-light looming on the wall behind him, his hankerchief still pressed to his mouth as he glanced fearfully about him. Holmes had us stand back by the wall, and beckoned forward Stamp. At a nod from Holmes, Stamp swung back his hammer and struck. The brickwork shook, and I felt through the soles of my boots the earthen floor shake. Again he struck, and again the brick wall shook, cracking this time, but still it held. At the third blow, the hammer crashed clean through. A cloud of black flies swarmed out into the cellar, accompanied by a foul stench, forcing us all to back away instantly; but Holmes soon came forward to the hole and, his hand covering his face, wrenched out a few more bricks. He called for the lantern, and I came forward, and held it up to the hole. We peered into the chimney space; in the swaying shadows and light it was possible to make out a corpse sitting on the floor of the cavity, its knees drawn up, chin on chest, crawling with maggots.

Flowerdew had already fled upstairs and could be heard vomiting outside the back door. Stamp and I came upstairs forthwith, brushing the flies away from our faces, and after a minute or so Holmes too came up. He locked the door to the cellar, summoned Mrs Stamp, and put her in charge of the house and her employer. Her husband was to take myself and Holmes to the railway station in the dog-cart. As soon as Stamp had harnessed the bay we seated ourselves and off we went. As we flew through the narrow lanes, Holmes pulled from his pocket a sheet of paper and contrived, despite the rocking and lurching of the carriage, to write out a message to Inspector Jones of Scotland Yard. When we drew up outside Mowl station, he gave it to Stamp, telling him to go to the local police station, alert them to the grisly discovery in the vicarage, and have them send the message immediately to Jones at the Yard. Away went Stamp, in a spray of mud from the wheels, and we turned to enter the railway station. I found upon enquiry that we had only some twenty minutes to wait for the next train to London. Standing on the platform, we naturally fell to discussing the strange and horrible turn the case had taken. I ventured to question the wisdom of our abrupt departure from the vicarage.

"No, no," said Holmes with a dismissive wave of his hand. " 'Let the dead bury their dead.' We can do nothing more here; we are needed at Camberwell now. Armstrong may return there at any hour; we must be ready and waiting for him. I hope that my note will reach the police in time for them to be with us at the end. I should prefer to have a constable or two at hand when we confront Mr Armstrong."

"Armstrong? The apprentice-master? What is his connection with the death of young Garrity?"

"That we shall soon know. There are a number of indications that he is intimately connected with the disappearance of the boy. For one thing, he alone was positive that the lad had been at Bromley. It seems that he was lying, and that when the Bromley job started, Garrity was in Great Mowl, bricked up in the cellar."

"Did you not tell me that Garrity's presence at Bromley was confirmed by the company's written records?"

"That means nothing. The records are written by Armstrong himself, and in his keeping. I already harboured some doubts about Armstrong, before we discovered the body. He was all hail-fellow-well-met with me, but speaking to the labourers and craftsmen led me to form a rather different picture of the man. They gave me the impression that beneath his bluster lay something more fearsome. It was hinted that he had nearly killed one of his men earlier in the year, and had contrived to keep the matter from the authorities, passing it off as an accident.

"Then Mrs Garrity's mysterious visitation of yesterday cast quite a different light on the matter, and raised a number of interesting questions. Why was her home ransacked immediately after I began my enquiries? Presumably someone had panicked when a private detective named Holmes came snooping round asking questions about Garrity's disappearance. What was the intruder looking for? It was clearly no ordinary burglary; nothing of value was taken. Perhaps he was hoping to abstract some damning piece of evidence from the Garrity appartment, and at the same time to suggest by the clumsy note that Garrity was still alive and well. Lastly, who was the intruder? For it was obviously not her son who ransacked the place. Ah, this is our train coming in, I think."

The London train pulled in to the platform, and we climbed aboard. Once we had found ourselves a compartment to ourselves Holmes pulled from his pocket a little notebook I had not seen before. For several minutes he leafed through it carefully without saying a word.

"Here, Watson, what do you make of this?" he finally asked, handing it to me. I opened it. Inside were rows and columns of figures written in pencil, headed 'price', 'quantity', 'del.', 'out', 'ret' etc. On the fly leaf was writtten *J. Garrity.*

"Good Lord, Holmes, this is the missing note-book! Where did you find it?"

'Indeed it is. I think even Inspector Jones will grasp the significance of this little item of evidence. I found it upon the poor boy's body, Watson, when I searched him an hour ago in the vicarage. It was in a small pocket in the lining of his pea-coat. Evidently Armstrong had overlooked it.'

"If he searched for it at all."

"Oh, he searched Garrity."

"How do you know, Holmes?"

"Because, when I searched the body just now, I did not find the boy's house-key. I found this note-book, a kerchief, a pencil, and some coins, but no key. Why not? Who fails to carry his house-key with him? Somebody had found it before me, and taken it. And later that person used it to enter Garrity's home. He was looking for something he never found, something incriminating. And what he was looking for, Watson, was this." With a gleam of triumph in his eyes, Holmes held aloft the little notebook.

The train, though a slow one, had the advantage to us of stopping at the Camberwell station. We soon arrived at Armstrong's office, or at least the passage that led to it, squeezed between two large, respectable establishments of the High Street. On its wooden gate was a large sign:

A Armstrong
Building Contractor

The gate being wide open, we walked down the passage to the end, where it opened out into a yard. On one side of this yard stood a kind of long, low hut. Holmes asked me to go back to the passage and stand guard there, while he went to see if Armstrong were inside the hut. In a few moments he returned, to report that there was only a clerk or accountant inside, going through some ledgers. There was no sign of Armstrong. We were standing there in the narrow defile, out of sight of Armstrong's office, debating how we might best prepare ourselves for his arrival, when two figures turned in from the street. For a moment they were silhouetted in the passage entrance, blocking our path, and then they moved towards us. My muscles tensed in readiness. Holmes was the first to speak.

"Ah, Inspector Jones, is it not?" he exclaimed. "I believe I had the pleasure of working with you in that business at Norwood. I take it my message reached you?"

"It did, Mr Holmes. I have brought with me constable Brummer" –who saluted each of us– "from the local station here. Brummer has just been telling me something of this fellow Armstrong and his cronies, which it might interest you to hear."

"Well, gentlemen," began the constable, "we know of Seth Armstrong at the station. We've known of him for a long time. He has never been convicted, mind you, nor even charged, but we've had our eye on him for years. As a young fellow he was a tearaway, forever fighting. He associated with a gang of felons operating here on the Surrey side of the river. We knew he was fencing for them, but we could never prove it. He was as slippery as an eel. Later, he did well in the building trade, and he opened his office, and now he's Mr Respectable Armstrong, and he dines with his worship the mayor, but he's still up to no good, we're pretty sure of that. Now he's older, he's fly enough to hide it, and that's about the size of it."

"He nearly succeeded in hiding his crime this time too," added Holmes. "Had my enquiries not precipitated him into an unnecessary burglary yesterday, he would almost certainly have escaped detection. But it seems that you'll have your Mr Armstrong at last, constable, if only we can hang on to him today."

It did not take long to decide on how we would receive Armstrong when he returned. Holmes, Jones and Brummer were to wait in his office, while I was to keep watch at the entrance to the passage. As someone who was neither uniformed nor known to him, I was thought least likely to raise any alarm in his mind. Once he was in the yard I would close and bolt the gate behind him.

Accordingly I took up my post in the little passage, skulking in the corner nearest the street, and observing Camberwell pass by in all its variety. In the meantime, as I afterwards learned, my fellows had entered the office and started to go through the company's books and records. Their searches were accompanied by protests from the secretary, but the burly presence of constable Brummer discouraged him from taking his protests any further. For myself, I had nothing to do but keep watch for Armstrong. I had been told to look for a large, red-faced man driving an open wagon pulled by a cob. Several hours passed, and I found myself on nodding terms with a couple of the local tradesmen at their doorsteps. Still my man did not appear. It was not until it was beginning to grow dark that at last I saw him coming down the road, a big man, standing high as he shook the reins. Having quickly flung a pebble at the office to warn my colleagues, I slipped out to the street to allow the wagon into the passage. I caught sight of Armstrong's face, heavy and crimson, as he jolted past; fortunately he was too intent on negotiating the narrow passage to notice me. Once in the yard, he jumped to the ground and marched into his office. Quick as I could, I shut the gate behind him, trapping him in the yard, and hurried to the office myself. As I reached the door a shout and a crash came from within. I entered to see the massive figure of Armstrong,

Jones hanging round his neck, staggering towards Holmes. With a violent wrench Armstrong flung the officer to the ground and closed in on Holmes. As he raised his arm to strike, constable Brummer seized it from behind. Armstrong gave a roar, and twisted round, but it was too late; the constable had him in an armlock. Armstrong was doubled up, still rolling and twisting to escape, when I heard the click of the handcuffs snapping shut. It was all over. Brummer manhandled Armstrong to his feet, and Jones, having got to his feet too, took the other side of Armstrong and informed him that he was under arrest for the wilful murder of James Garrity.

That evening Holmes and I were back in our Baker Street flat. I picked up the newspaper. Famine in India, revolt in Africa; the greatest statesmen of the land confronting each other in the House; a scandal in the London theatre: these were the topics of the moment. How far they seemed from what we had uncovered that day. Would the murder of a builder's apprentice make such a noise in the great world? I wondered.

"One aspect of the affair escapes me, Holmes. I am still puzzled as to the motive behind the murder of Garrity. Why did Armstrong kill him? And what was the significance of the notebook, that Armstrong risked everything trying to retrieve it?"

"Ah yes, the notebook. That little notebook is the key to the whole affair. As you know, it contains all the details of Armstrong's building supplies. On a cursory examination it seems to be of little interest. You saw it yourself, Watson; long and tedious lists of goods, dates and prices of sale, deliveries, and so on. A careful reading of it reveals something much more interesting, though, as I discovered on the train back to Camberwell this afternoon. During the journey I had time to examine some of the entries carefully and collate them with each other, and a most fascinating picture emerged: a long history of materials ordered and paid for but not delivered, materials vanishing inexpicably, materials appearing unordered and not paid for, payments for non-existent goods – in short, the detailed account of systematic fraud practised by Armstrong. He must have been horrified to find that evidence of his dishonesty had been so carefully recorded, and on his own instructions. It cannot have occurred to him, when he instructed his apprentice to keep lists of the materials, that his young assistant would prove so thorough a book-keeper. Did Armstrong perhaps try to bribe or threaten the lad, and find himself rebuffed? Did Garrity threaten to inform the police, or Armstrong's cheated clients? We will never know. In any event, at the end of the job at Great Mowl vicarage, when most of the tradesmen and labourers were elsewhere, a confrontation of some kind took place between the two, and Armstrong struck the boy a mortal blow. Suddenly he found he had a body on his hands, but the resourceful brute quickly lit on a place to hide it. Partly dismantling the wall he had built only a few days before in front of the cellar boiler, he stuffed Garrity's body behind it. First he rifled the boy's pockets, but the notebook lay hidden in an inner pocket of the coat, and Armstrong in his haste failed to find it. He must have guessed it to be in Garrity's rooms, and have therefore taken the house key from the pocket, planning to retrieve the book when lad's mother was out. He rebuilt the damaged wall with the corpse now behind it, knowing that the stench of the body as it rotted would rise up the flue and remain undetected. Armstrong left the vicarage, leaving behind, as he thought, his dead apprentice, safely bricked in. But the poor lad, although too weak to escape from his immolation, was not quite dead. He lived on behind the furnace for a week or more, his dying moans, heard by the Stamps above, taken for the noises of a ghost."

The Case of the Quiet Crescent

SHERLOCK HOLMES STOOD by the window of our Baker Street flat, peering closely at a small envelope. Round and round he turned it in his long fingers, scrutinising it from different angles; he held it up to the light; he sniffed at it; finally he flung it over to me. "What do you make of it, Watson?"

Years of assisting in his enquiries had given me the opportunity to observe his methods, and I did my best to follow them now. The envelope was cream-coloured and lightly scented. "Written by a woman," I concluded. "Not a rich woman – nor poor." I noticed the franking on the stamp: "Ah! It was posted in the NW district this morning." At this point inspiration deserted me.

"You deduce the lady's financial state from the quality of the envelope, I take it. I agree with you. The quality of the perfume – an artificial synthesis in imitation of Parma violet – might have led you to the same conclusion."

"Did I miss anything?" I asked.

"Only that the lady is self-possessed and precise in nature, that she is probably single and in daily employment, and that the matter on which she writes does not directly concern her."

"Do you really learn all that from the envelope, Holmes?"

"I suppose you want an explanation, Watson, don't you, so that you can shrug your shoulders and tell me how childishly simple my deductions were. Let me oblige you. The self-possession is evinced by the lady's hand, which, although she has sufficient occasion to turn to a private detective, remains clear and unhurried. It is a hand that proclaims neatness too, of course, as does the placing of the stamp."

"Holmes, we all stick the stamp in the top right-hand corner."

"And we all have the same number of limbs and bodily organs in the same places, doctor. Are your patients therefore all identical? Do you skate over their symptoms with scarcely a second glance? Look again!" He thrust the envelope back into my hands. "I tell you, Watson, I could write a sizeable monograph on the placement of stamps upon envelopes. There are stamps like cornered rats backed up against the very edges of the envelope, stamps sallying forth halfway into the middle of the envelope, stamps at rakish angles, carefully aligned stamps – then there are the thumbprints on them, greasy or grimy, the not-quite-stuck-down stamps peeling up at the corner – and how are they taken from the sheet? Some are removed carefully along the perforations, others hurriedly torn so a corner is ripped off. There are still a few to be seen that have been cut from the sheet with scissors. They all have something to tell. Well, look at this one. You see it has no rips, no oddities of position, no dirty thumbprints – everything about it suggests that the lady is neat, balanced and self-possessed.

"What were the other points? Ah yes; let us take firstly her being employed. That I deduce from the hour the letter was posted; shortly before eight in the morning, when she may have been on her way to work. That is only supposition, of course, but few ladies of leisure, I think, would be posting their correspondence at that hour. Her single state I deduce in turn from her being in employment. Another supposition, therefore; dear me, what loose habits of thought I seem to be slipping into! That the matter does not directly concern the lady I infer partly from the calmness I have already mentioned, and partly from the fact of her writing a letter. She would surely have called in person or sent a telegram had the matter been pressing."

"The matter might not be pressing and yet be her own case," I countered.

"Very correct, Watson! So it might; but the likelihood, I think, is as I suggest. Pressing troubles are usually one's own; it is those of others that can wait. Well, we have examined the envelope. Let us now look inside." He picked up the paper-knife, opened the envelope with a flourish, and took out a single sheet of note-paper.

" 'Mr Sherlock Holmes,' " he read, " 'I beg you will forgive my writing to you, but I am at a loss to know where to turn for help. I am alarmed by recent events here in Belford Crescent. Had I not witnessed them myself, I should have said they were impossible. I will call on you on Thursday morning at ten o'clock, if I do not inconvenience you.

Yours truly

Miss Rose Davies'

"Well, Watson, we have had the grotesque, the bizarre, and the mysterious, over the years, but I think this is the first time that we have been promised the impossible. I shall be interested to see what it is like. The lady does not allow us much time; she will be here within an hour. Will you stay for her visit?"

"I should very much like to. I wonder what it is that brings her here? 'The impossible' – what on earth can that mean?"

"We have already speculated enough on Miss Rose Davies and her visit, I think; there seems little point in further speculation, since the lady herself will be here in an hour's time. I propose to spend that hour profitably, if tediously, in updating my card-index." So saying, he pulled out one of the boxes in which the index was housed, and fell to work. Sherlock Holmes was possessed of extraordinary powers of concentration that enabled him to focus his attention fully on any task in hand, ignoring all distractions, and he was, accordingly, still engrossed in his indexing when at ten o'clock precisely the street-bell sounded, followed immediately by a tap on our door.

"Come!" cried Holmes.

A lady of some twenty-five summers entered. She looked about her with quick grey eyes. "Mr Sherlock Holmes?" she asked.

"I am Sherlock Holmes, Miss Davies," he answered with a bow, adding, in response to her glance at me, "and this is my friend Dr Watson. Be seated, I beg you."

"Thank you, Mr Holmes. It is very good of you to see me. I know you are a busy man. Our concerns may seem trivial to you, and indeed I do not wish to waste your time, but I did not know to whom I could turn."

"I shall be pleased to help if I can, Miss Davies. Now, pray tell me about the impossible events that have led you to my door."

"I shall be as brief as I may be, Mr Holmes," the young lady began, but Holmes interrupted her immediately. "Miss Davies, you are right to say that I am a busy man. You are busy too, I see; you know that time is valuable, and I am confident that you will not waste my time or your own. Please do not trouble yourself on that account. You have arranged to be absent from your work this morning, I take it?"

"I have."

"Then we have two hours or more at our disposal. I beg you therefore to tell me your story fully. Omit no detail that may be of importance."

"Thank you." Miss Davies paused for a few seconds, arranging her thoughts, and then began her narrative. "I am a teacher's assistant in St Mark's School in Kentish Town. On taking up the post two terms ago I took lodgings in Belford Crescent nearby. My rooms are small, but pleasant, and convenient for the school. I have been content enough there. It is a quiet, respectable little street, not a place where anything much out of the way ever happens – not until recently, that is.

"Three weeks ago – two Wednesdays before yesterday – it was a holiday, and I was not needed at school. Late in the morning, at about eleven o'clock, I went out to buy my groceries, and as I left the house I passed two men standing on the pavement. One was a taller man, of your height, perhaps, and the other was a short, dark-skinned man, a little older than myself. I noticed, though I thought little of it at the time, that the short man wore a red flannel waistcoat with brass buttons to it. As they stood there talking to each other I passed them and walked to the end of the street, which is only a short way, and round the corner to the greengrocer's. There outside the greengrocer's stood the short, dark man, in his red waistcoat. He could not have passed me, Mr Holmes, without my seeing him, for the street was empty, and there is no shorter way to the greengrocer's than the way I went. No cabs or carriages had passed in the road. I bought my vegetables in a daze, wondering how the man could have been transported instantly and invisibly past me. I wondered if perhaps I had imagined him, and if I was overstrained at work and becoming ill. You hear of people who end their days in an insane asylum.

"The week after, something else unaccountable took place in our street. They have a maid next door who sometimes comes round to share a pot of tea with me. Poor dear, she is not long up from the country, and she misses her folk terribly. She feels herself friendless in London. A fortnight ago she told me of a very strange thing that had happened in her house that had frightened her. A business friend of her master's had called to see him. She knew her master was at home, in the parlour, because she heard him playing the piano as she went to the front door to answer the doorbell. But when she knocked on the parlour door there was no answer. She opened the door and there was no-one in the room. He could not have left the parlour without her noticing, as its door is just by the front door. She had had the strange idea, she told me, that perhaps her master had not wanted to see his visitor and was hiding behind the sofa. She returned to the front door to tell the caller that Mr Harfield was not at home. The caller left, but moments later, looking out of the parlour window, she saw her master and his visitor talking together on the pavement. It made her feel dazed, she said, and troubled. I told her of my own experience with the dark little man, which had left me feeling just as she had felt, and she told me that she had seen the short dark man too, at the other end of the street. She had wondered if he was an organ-grinder.

The next time I went to the greengrocer's I asked about the organ-grinder, as I called him. The greengrocer told me that the man had been in his shop several times. On most days he was not to be seen, but occasionally he would be there a number of times in one day, in and out of the shop, buying a pound of this or that, or loafing about in the street."

"Was he an old customer?" asked Holmes.

"No, the greengrocer told me that this had only been going on for a few weeks. When I went to the dairy I was told the same thing – the organ-grinder had suddenly appeared one day, loafing around to no purpose, apparently. Then he had disappeared for a week or so, only to reappear again. All the shopkeepers had noticed it."

"This is most interesting, Miss Davies. When was this mysterious stranger last seen in Belford Crescent?"

"Last Monday, so far as I know. But as I am at work during the day, I am less likely to see him than some."

"And what does he do, apart from lounge about?"

"Nothing, as far as anyone has seen. None of us has been able to guess at the reason for his erratic visits."

"I see." Sherlock Holmes sank back into his chair, closed his eyes, and putting his hands palms together, raised them to his lips like one in prayer. He maintained this priestly attitude for some time, and his eyes were still closed when finally he lowered his hands and spoke:

"Your friend of next door, the maid; has she had any other strange experiences? Experiences like the music she heard from the empty room two weeks ago, I mean?"

Miss Davies shook her head. "Who knows? I'm not sure that she would tell me if she had. But I do know that she is unhappy and frightened. I can see it so clearly in her sad, anxious face, even if she does not speak about it. Yesterday she asked the doctor if he could give her something for her nerves, but he declined."

"Her anxieties were acute enough to make her visit her doctor," I interjected.

"Oh no, Dr Watson, she did not visit her doctor. This was the doctor of her mistress Miss Harfield, on a house visit. He attends Miss Harfield regularly at her home. She suffers badly from her nerves."

"Does she, indeed?" said Holmes. "There seems quite an epidemic of nervous disorder in Belford Crescent. Perhaps the condition is contagious. The household next door to you seems a rather strange and unhappy one. What can you tell me about your neighbours of yours?"

"Miss Harfield has lived in the house for about four years, they say, and her brother moved in not long before I took my rooms next door to them at number fifty-nine."

"He joined his sister a little less than a year ago, then?"

"That is right, Mr Holmes. Mr Rupert Harfield is a man of several business interests, about which I can tell you nothing beyond the fact that they bring a number of callers to his door, men of various types. He is about forty years old, affable enough, even familiar in manner – a brisk and busy man. I believe that is quite usual among men of affairs. Miss Harfield, his sister, is a shy person, pale in complexion. I have seen her less and less as her health has deteriorated; she is not confined to bed or physically infirm, but her neurasthenia has made it very difficult for her to leave her home. She ventures out about twice a week now, the maid tells me, to sit in the park, or make some small purchases. The Harfields have a cook and housekeeper to look after the running of the household. I have not been inside the house, but I can tell you what Aggie, the Harfields' maid, has told me. It is not an easy or friendly place, by her account. She is uncomfortable with some of Mr Harfield's acquaintances, and her mistress's ill health causes her unease. When she started to work there, before Mr Harfield joined his sister, her mistress, though frail and a little nervous, was friendly, and would sometimes chat to Aggie. Now Miss Harfield, if she so much as passes Aggie on the stairs, starts like a hare or slinks past with her head down. It is like working for a ghost, is how Aggie put it to me. As for Mr Harfield, although Aggie has made it clear that she has no real grounds for complaint against him, she dislikes his arbitrary rules, and she has found to her cost that an infringement of them can make him unreasonably angry."

"Did she give you any examples of what she meant by that?"

"Yes, she did. Let me tell you. Mr Harfield is an amateur pianist, and when playing did not like to be interrupted by the maid or his sister or anyone else."

Holmes raised an eyebrow. "I have some sympathy for the man."

"As do I, Mr Holmes," replied Miss Davies with a smile, "and at first Aggie too was entirely happy with the arrangement. If possible, she would wait until her master had finished playing before she entered the room, and if she needed to enter the room she would not interrupt him. If she carried a message from his sister, for instance, or there was a caller at the door, she would wait silently until he was ready to hear her. That arrangement changed, however. A month ago her employer told her that if he was in the parlour playing the piano she should on no account enter. Well, it was only about a week later that a caller came to the door asking for her master, insisting that it was a matter of great urgency. She could hear Mr Harfield playing in the parlour, and tapped lightly at the door. There being no response, she turned the handle, when she heard a roar of "Get out!" accompanied by an oath. The music stopped suddenly and her master flung open the door. Black in the face with rage, he ordered her to her room and told her that if she disobeyed his orders again she would be dismissed instantly. The poor girl fled upstairs in tears, and although he subsequently resumed his casually agreeable manner with her, the episode left her unhappy, wondering when his foul temper would flare up again without warning."

"Thank you," said Holmes. "You have painted us a very clear picture of your neighbours' household in Belford Crescent. I fear it would be too much to hope that you have any clear recollection of the dates of these events."

"Not entirely," came her answer. "I have done my best to remember the dates." She opened her handbag and took out a folded sheet of paper. "I have written them out as as well as I could."

"Miss Davies, you are a model client. May I keep the paper?"

"Of course."

"I have one last question for you. Do you feel that you are in danger?"

"I am not quite sure how to answer you," she said as she closed her bag. She pondered for a few seconds. "I shall say this: I don't think that I myself am threatened, but I sense the presence of danger."

Holmes nodded. He rose from his chair and started to pace the room. "I am very grateful to you for bringing this curious problem to my attention, Miss Davies. I shall certainly look into it. Would it be convenient for me to come to you in Belford Crescent in a day or two?"

"I should be very grateful, Mr Holmes. The school day finishes at noon on Saturday; I shall be free at any time after noon."

"I shall call on you at one o'clock. In the meantime, perhaps you will be able to help me. I should like to know of any other strange events that may have occurred in Belford Crescent similar to those you have described; talk to your neighbours' maid, if you would, and to any other of your acquaintances in the crescent, and we shall see if any further details emerge."

Miss Davies rose and put on her hat and gloves. "Thank you. It is a great relief to me know that you will be looking into this affair." She extended her hand. "Goodbye, Dr Watson, and Mr Holmes."

It so happened that some private business of my own required my presence elsewhere on the next day, when my friend was to visit Belford Crescent, so I was unable to accompany him. I much regretted the circumstance, for it always gave me keen pleasure to help Sherlock Holmes in an enquiry, but there was nothing to be done. It was not until the following Tuesday, almost a week after Miss Davies' visit, that I saw Holmes again. We had just enjoyed an excellent luncheon provided for us by Mrs Hudson, and were taking our ease in the well-worn comfortable chairs of our Baker Street rooms, legs stretched before us. We lit our pipes and for some minutes smoked in contented silence. "What a strange set of circumstances that young woman Rose Davies was telling us about," I said. "Do you think you'll get to the bottom of it?"

Holmes took his pipe from his mouth: "It is too early to say. Certainly I am not there yet. It's a strange case indeed, and a sinister one. The bottom lies a long way down, I fear."

"You visited Miss Davies?"

"Yes. Most illuminating it was. I had asked her, if you remember, to sound out her neighbours for more facts, and they obliged with two new pieces of information. The first was, to be more precise, the confirmation of an old piece of information, that very peculiar business of the miraculously reappearing organ-grinder. The postman told her of a similar experience. It happened on a late morning delivery, at about eleven o'clock. He had started at one end of Belford Crescent, and when he reached the other end, having finished his deliveries for the street, he saw the organ-grinder, complete with his brass-buttoned waistcoat. The postman thought nothing of it, naturally, but he gave the fellow good-day, and his greeting was returned. At that moment he found in his bag a misplaced letter intended for the other end of the Belford Crescent, where he had started his delivery. He was obliged to retrace his steps quickly; and when he reached the other end, there to his astonishment was the organ-grinder again. When he nodded good-day to him again, the man feigned not to know him. The postman swore it was the same man in the same waistcoat, and was in no doubt that the man could not possibly have overtaken him without his knowledge. The postman had not mentioned the matter to anyone, as he did not want to gain a reputation for weakness of mind or drunkenness.

"The second piece of information Miss Davies gleaned from her friend the maid. The maid had been sitting in her attic room when she thought she heard a male voice, distinct and unpleasant, repeating accusations and suggestions in a sneering tone of voice. The voice sounded close, and clear, but with something of an echo, like a voice in an empty church. There was nobody on the same floor as the maid, and no man in the house. The only other person in the house at the time was her mistress, and she was on the ground floor. Naturally enough, this episode, coming as it did after the piano being played in the empty room, greatly disconcerted the poor girl. She feared that either the house was haunted or that she was going mad.

"As Miss Davies spoke with the maid another odd episode from the recent past emerged. Aggie had overheard a conversation between Miss Harfied and a friend – "

"I thought she had no friends who visited her?" I interrupted.

"Not now, no," replied Holmes. "But the maid was talking of a year or so ago, when the lady was less isolated. She had overheard the two ladies talking. 'I can't have them here,' Miss Harfield had said. 'I don't know where they have come from.'

Aggie did not know what to make of this remark, but she was to remember it later, because the night after she had heard the conversation she was woken by sounds of movement in the house. It was in the early hours of the morning, long after everyone had retired to bed. She

135

crept out of her room, and without a candle came out onto the landing of her attic room. It was too dark to see, but she could hear people moving on the stairs below her. Occasionally there was a muffled whisper. From the voices and the weight of footsteps on the stairs she was sure the figures were men, perhaps three of them. Fearful of confronting the burglars, if burglars they were, she went back into her room and looked out of her dormer window, which overlooks the street. It was a black, moonless night, but she could just make out a cab outside the house. Its lights were not burning. Some figures emerged slowly from the house and climbed into the cab, which drove away. Nothing about the episode was said in the house the following day, and when the maid hinted to her mistress that something amiss might have occurred during the night, her suggestion was met with a firm denial.

"This new information was most suggestive, but I was mindful that the purpose of my visit had been to make sense of the weird events Miss Davies had told us about, not to collect further instances of them. Very well; how was I to explain them? Everything seemed to centre on the Harfield home, and I decided that my first step should be to pay it a visit and see for myself this mysterious menage. Miss Davies, however, was sure that the maid, in her extremely nervous state, would not wish to admit me, and Miss Harfield herself was by now almost a recluse and even more unlikely to allow me entry. Foreseeing these difficulties, I had brought with me the outfit of a delivery man, and thus disguised I knocked at the tradesmen's door bearing a brown-paper parcel. The maid, Aggie, admitted me and took me into the scullery to leave the parcel. I insisted, however, that the item must be fitted by me to the piano, and she accordingly took me into the parlour. At this moment Miss Davies, by prior arrangement, knocked at the door for Aggie, begging her to come with her on some pretext. She was splendidly insistent, and the poor maid could not resist being drawn away from her duties. Once they had gone I examined the room. I first opened the piano, and found something most interesting inside. Perhaps you have already guessed, Watson?"

"I can't say that I have."

"I found that it had been converted to a pianola."

"One of those new devices that plays the piano automatically, like a music-box?"

"Exactly. In a cupboard were a number of piano rolls, one of which I took and secreted in my delivery bag. I also helped myself to a cigar from the box, and the butt of a cigar from the fireplace. I was determined to take a look at Miss Harfield's room if I could, but I had little time, for I did not know for how much longer Miss Davies would be able to distract the maid, and furthermore I might at any point run into the house-keeper or Miss Harfield herself. I hurried up the stairs, and as I stood on the landing the door before me opened and a most distraught lady, wan and trembling, came out. She looked at me in astonishment. 'Afternoon, Ma'am,' I said. 'Here to check the fitting, begging your pardon.' I touched my forehead and without waiting for her permission entered the room she had just left. On top of a chest of drawers stood a range of phials and bottles. Above the chest, as luck would have it, was a gas lamp. As I fiddled with the lamp, my back to the lady, I managed to drop a number of the bottles into my satchell. 'Thanking you, ma'am,' I said as I saluted her and went back down the stairs. The poor lady – it was Miss Harfield, of course – never uttered a word. As I reached the bottom of the stairs I heard a door at the back of the house closing, and the footsteps of the maid advancing down the back hall. Just in time I got back to the parlour. When the maid entered, I pointed out that the label was badly written and that the parcel was in fact for Belford Close, not Belford Crescent. Grumbling about the office wasting my time, I made my way out, the parcel under my arm, but before I left I took the precaution of asking her not to mention the wrong delivery to her employers, as I didn't want to lose my position.

"My next task was to examine the roof of the Harfield house."

"The roof?" I wondered. "What made you want to look at the roof?"

"The voice that the maid had heard, Watson. Where do you suppose it had come from?"

"I hadn't asked myself that question, but now you raise it, I can't say the roof is the answer that springs immediately to mind. Was not the voice perhaps in the mind of the maid? Perhaps she had fallen asleep momentarily and dreamed it."

"It is most unlike you, Watson, to suggest a mental explanation in preference to a physical one. I fear that I lack your newly ethereal cast of mind; I took a more prosaic approach, and asked myself where the voice had come from. The most likely answer, if I may beg to differ from you, was that it had come down the chimney."

I felt no inclination to be browbeaten by my friend's mocking tone.

"Oh!" I said. "Of course. Some fellow wishing to speak to the maid, instead of ringing the bell, naturally strolled up to the roof and bellowed down the chimney at her. How dull I have been."

Holmes raised his eyebrows and smiled. "Touché! I underestimated the sharpness of your tongue, Watson. I must be more careful in future. It would indeed have been a rather unusual way to address the maid, but you forget, perhaps, that few chimneys serve only one fireplace. The chimney for Aggie's fireplace also serves that of Miss Harfield, who (according to the maid, *per* Miss Davies) passes a good deal of the day in her room. I suspect that the evil words were intended for her ears."

"I suppose that's a possibility," I conceded, "but why would someone wish to insult the lady secretly in that way? Do you suppose some feud, some bad blood between her and this man on the roof?"

"Why indeed? That is an excellent question, my boy, and one that lies at the heart of this enquiry. But you know my views on trying to build theories on insufficient facts. We will do better first to lay out clearly before us such facts as we have, and only then to try to account for them. So before addressing your question, I will continue with my account of such facts as I was able to discover yesterday. So, back to the roof: luckily Miss Davies's rooms give access to a loft, whose skylight enabled me to climb onto the roof itself. Thence I crossed onto the roof of the neighbouring house, the Harfields'. Near their chimney I found unmistakeable signs of activity. There were fresh scratches in the sooty lip of the chimney itself; corners had been recently chipped off two of the slates at the foot of the stack; the dust and debris that accumulated there had been recently disturbed, although it was all too dry for anything so definite as a footprint; I found some cigar ash, and in the guttering nearby the butt of a cigar. I then crawled over to the Harfields' skylight; it had been recently opened."

Holmes went over to the table and fished out from under a pile of discarded newspapers and other clutter some matchboxes. They were labelled in his neat hand. "Here," he said, opening one of them and passing it to me, "is the cigar butt I found on the roof. This," he continued, opening another, "is the butt from the parlour." He passed me his magnifying lens. "Compare them. Notice particularly how the end has been cut on each." They were indeed almost identical. "I shall smoke the fresh cigar later," he continued, "and compare its ash with the ash I found on the roof."

"There seems no doubt that your conjecture about the chimney was correct. Someone was up there. You think it was the man Harfield?"

"Either he or someone smoking one of his cigars."

"I am bound to agree with you, Holmes, that the business begins to take on a criminal aspect. I thought it merely bizarre at first, I admit. Did you make any headway over the organ-grinder?" I asked. "His impossible movements seem to me the most mystifying of all the strange events in Belford Crescent."

"I made two small discoveries, although far from constituting an advance, they merely confirm the difficulty of explaining the matter. Firstly, as I was telling you, the milkman confirmed Miss Davies' story. That is important, for it means we can put aside any idea that the organ-grinder and his strange movements are a figment of her imagination. Secondly, I was able to establish that there was no short cut from one end of Belford Crescent to the other, no ready access from the street to the houses' back gardens, nothing that would screen one person in the street from another; so the conundrum of his supernatural speed remains unexplained."

"You have no indication how it was done, or why?"

"I have an idea, but it is not yet tested; if it turns out to be more than mere fancy, you shall know of it. For the moment, I have more practical business on hand than the airing of unsubstantiated theories. I must make some inquiries into the affairs of the Harfield household. I was hoping that you might be able to help me."

"I hope so too. I am less busy this week than last, now that my neighbour has returned."

"Excellent!" Holmes sprang to his feet and brought over a large cylinder from the table. "This is the purloined piano-roll. I take it you have no fixed objection to handling stolen goods? You see here the name of the maker: Peter Schelling, London, NW. Would you be good enough, Watson, to visit Mr Schelling, and find out what you can? You might claim to be an acquaintance of Harfield, so impressed with his mechanical piano that you are desirous of some similar device yourself. Find out what you can about Harfield and the piano rolls. In the meantime I shall see what I can find out about Mr Rupert Harfield himself, his business interests and his shadowy sister."

"I shall go to see this Schelling fellow tomorrow morning." Although Holmes had satisfied my curiosity about the facts of the case, as far as he was able to, I was convinced that he understood more of what lay behind those facts than he had divulged. It was always his way to play his cards close to his chest, but I could not forebear to try him a little further. More in hope than expectation I asked him whether he thought the unusual events in Belford Crescent were connected, and if so what he thought that connection might be, what motive or purpose might lie behind them.

"As to what happened, you know as much as I. You heard Miss Davies' account, and of my subsequent findings I have hidden nothing from you. As to why these things happened, I suggest you ask yourself this question: what effect did the mysterious organ-grinder, the piano music, and the voice in the chimney have on those who witnessed them?"

I could press my friend no further. With that decisiveness of attention that was such a marked aspect of his character he said no more, but took up his violin and bow. Evidently the discussion of events in Belford Crescent was over. He coaxed strange sounds from the instrument, not music, perhaps, so much as the expression of thoughts beyond the reach of speech, unearthly sounds that might as easily have originated on the moon as on this planet. It came as a relief to me when after some time he turned to something less alien, and played some pieces he knew to be amongst my favourites, some German *lieder* and a few folk-songs of our own country. With these familiar harmonies the afternoon drew to a close.

The next morning I set out for the offices of Schelling with the piano-roll under my arm. The company's premises were in a street by the Regent's Park. The shop was large, dark, and furnished with some half-dozen pianos. A bell had tinkled in the distance as I entered, and eventually a young man appeared. I showed him the roll.

"It belongs to an acquaintance of mine, Mr Harfield of Kentish Town," I said. "I wonder if you might be able to tell me about this roll. I am interested in buying something similar that would play some of my own favourite pieces."

"May I see it? Ah, I thought so. This roll was made by us for your friend. A special order. One moment, if you please."

He opened the door by which he had just entered and shouted down: "Mr Ludo, an enquiry about rolls!"

A muffled reply came up, which I could not make out. "Would you be kind enough to follow me, sir?" asked the assistant, and led me through the back of the shop and down a flight of stairs to a large low room full of pianos and parts of pianos. My guide knocked at one of several doors and a guttural voice behind it called out "Come!"

I entered a small workshop, lit from a window at pavement level. In appearance and in smell it was something between a printer's workshop and a cabinet-maker's. A man of some fifty years in a cotton apron came forward. "Good morning, sir," he said. "Ah, you have one roll of mine, I see. Is there problem?"

"No problem at all, Mr . ."

"My name is Knapp."

"The roll is quite satisfactory, Mr Knapp. I wanted to ask you if you might be able to make some similar rolls for myself. This was made for Mr Harfield."

Knapp took the cylinder in one hand and with the other unrolled a yard of it like a scroll, holding it upright. He peered at the many little rectangular perforations that dotted the length of paper. "This is unusual – some repeats come at wrong time, I think. Let us listen." He rolled it back up and went through another door. "Come, sir, come!" he called, and I followed him. In the back room was an upright piano stripped of its casing. It contained not only the usual mechanisms of harp-like strings, hammers and dampers, but also a complicated arrangement of valves attached to a leather bag and of cords attached to the hammers. Knapp was fitting the end of the roll to a spool in the piano. He straightened up: "Now, we shall hear, no?"

He threw a switch. The machinery moved into action, swifter than the eye could follow, and the music came forth. I had heard something of piano rolls, but I had for some reason expected that the mechanism would bypass the keys; it was a disconcerting sight to see them rise and fall in succession as if an invisible player was at the instrument. After only a few bars Knapp threw the switch and everything stopped. "You heard, sir? He makes mistake, then plays it again correct, and again, so then continues." He wound the roll back manually and turned to me with his forefinger raised. "Listen!"

He switched on again, and just as he had said, a phrase was falsely played, then corrected, played again, and the piece continued. "You understand?"

"I think I do. The music is not played perfectly; the mistakes the pianist made are preserved."

"Yes! Yes! So, I remember now this man your friend." He hurried back to the room we had just come from, picked up the roll's case and consulted something written on it. "Here is number," he muttered to himself, and opened a drawer in a cabinet. He flicked through the cards, pulled out the one he was searching for, and read from it:

"HARFIELD Mr Rupert, of 57 Belford Crescent, London. Self recording, 8 August 98, 8 rolls

"I remember this occasion. Your friend plays piano and

I record eight rolls, mistakes and everything. I can make mistakes to vanish, I can cut holes for missing note, I can cover holes for note that is wrong, but this he does not want, he wants with mistakes."

"I dare say that is unusual."

"Yes, unusual, most people want it to play perfect."

"How interesting. Did my friend Harfield tell you why he wanted the mistakes kept in?"

"Yes, he was telling me about his theatre, that is why he needed mistakes."

"I don't understand."

"He has theatre play where sometimes one actor must play piano, but he cannot play piano, so he pretend, and piano play itself. But Mr Harfield, he is clever, he say to himself, if it play too good, nobody believe, they know it is not real, so he play it himself here, and we keep mistakes, so it is like real when it plays on stage."

I seemed to have gathered all I usefully could from Mr Knapp. I asked a few more questions about piano rolls, and we agreed that ready-made rolls were cheaper and, for my purposes, better. I told him how helpful he had been – which I felt with some shame was almost the only true word I had spoken to the honest fellow – and went upstairs. There I was treated to a lecture from the assistant about the types of machinery used to play piano rolls, until I finally shook myself free of him, and, my head swimming with the details of peripheral pneumatics and isolators, I returned to Baker Street.

I was alone there, and was pleased to be able to read up in one of the medical journals on some recent advances in anaesthetics. After an hour or so Mr Sherlock Holmes breezed into the room, flinging his hat upon the table, and himself into the bath chair. He lit a cigarette. "Well,

Watson, how did you fare in your enquiries?"

I told him what I had learnt, the news of which seemed to delight him.

"This confirms my speculations on what lies behind these unaccountable events in Belford Crescent. I don't suppose you thought to check on Harfield's story of the play?"

"I didn't. Is it important?"

I must confess that I was a little disappointed to hear my friend's question. Try though I might, my researches on his behalf never seemed to satisfy him.

"Come, Watson, don't be downhearted. What you have found is invaluable. Since you ask me, however, I must say that it would of course be better to check on the veracity of this story about the theatre. Could you check on it later this afternoon? You would do me a great service. Of course I would do it myself, but I am fully engaged on other matters."

"Yes, I suppose I could do so. I am covered at the practice today by my neighbour."

"Excellent! I rely upon you."

"I hope you can, but I am not at all sure how to go about checking on Harfield's story."

"A good theatrical agent will be able to help you. He will know all about what was happening on the London stage that summer. I should tell you, by the way, that Harfield does have some theatrical connections, so his story is very likely true. Now, I have other business this afternoon that will not wait." He picked up his hat and walking-cane. "Good luck with your enquiries, Watson. I expect our paths will cross again this evening."

Following the advice of my friend I visited a theatrical agent, Nathaniel Rezin, in his office in the West end of

London. In the little ante-chamber where I waited, the office-boy told me that he thought it unlikely Mr Rezin would see me without an appointment; but when I gave my card with a note scribbled on it to the effect that I was acting for my friend Sherlock Holmes, I was straightaway admitted to Rezin's office. He recognised the name of Harfield, as having been involved with the staging of some productions a few years ago, and asked me if I was proposing to become involved with Harfield in the way of business; when I answered no, he nodded, as if reassured. I then told him what, according to Knapp, Harfield had said about the piano roll, and its use on the stage. Mr Rezin looked me directly in the eye. "You are asking me if I think the piano rolls were used for the purpose you described?"

"That is what I am asking," I confirmed.

"I do not think that they were," he answered in his soft voice. "I will tell you why. In the first place, a reproducing piano is not a cheap item, and I can assure you that every theatre manager wishes to lay out as little money as he can upon his productions. In the second place, actors able to play the piano come ten a penny. In the third place, most theatres boast a piano in the pit, which would serve the purpose equally well. And in the fourth place, I recollect no production at the time you mention in which one of the characters plays a piano onstage."

"Well, Mr Rezin, that seems quite conclusive."

Again he nodded.

"That is all I need to know," I said, "and as you are a busy man I shall not detain you longer. It has been kind of you to give me your time."

That evening Holmes and I were together in our Baker

Street rooms. It was late, and the shutters had long been closed and the lamps lit. Holmes seemed tired, but he revived his energies with a glass of brandy-and-water, and soon his eyes burned again with the heat of the chase. I took a glass myself, and we talked over the discoveries of the day. I repeated to him the opinion Mr Rezin had given me.

"Ah, so Harfield's reasons for using piano-rolls were not what he claimed," said he. "I thought as much."

"Of course, his reasons may have been innocent ones."

"That is hardly likely, Watson. Certainly Harfield himself does not seem to have thought them innocent, since he lied about them."

"True enough," I admitted. "Rezin did not say it in so many words, but I had the impression that he did not think Harfield a man of sound character."

Holmes gave a derisive snort. "I should think he did not. What I have discovered today about Mr Rupert Harfield suggests a man of the most dubious sort. Touch him where you will, he is rotten, rotten to the core."

"What did you find out about him?"

"I shall tell you, if I might trouble you first for another glass of brandy-and-water. Thank you. Well, Old Harfield, the father of Mr Rupert and his sister Miss Matilda – there were no other children, by the way – was a Bristol lawyer who by a combination of hard work and business acumen became a wealthy man. The mother died when the children were young, and Harfield never remarried. In fact he became something of a recluse, dividing his life exclusively between his work and his investments, with little time left over to spend on his children. In time Rupert went up to the University, which he left with no degree but considerable debts. In the space of a few years he formed several limited companies, none of which flourished, and most of which were dissolved leaving disappointed investors and creditors. With this talent for losing money he combined expensive tastes, and he ran up large accounts with his tailor, his vintners, and other tradesmen. His sister Matilda, meanwhile, took an opposite course. She lived modestly at her father's house, and spent little. Her only indulgence seems to have taken the form of two annual cheques, one made out to Archbishop Speke's Mission to Borneo and the other to the Animals' Friends' Society. Brother and sister each received an annual allowance from old Harfield; as you may suppose, Matilda's was more than enough for her, while Rupert's scarcely affected his ever-growing debts. Four years ago the old man died; the house was sold, and the entire estate was shared equally between brother and sister. Miss Matilda bought a house in North London, invested the remaining capital and lived comfortably on the interest. Mr Rupert spent more than ever, lost more than ever in ill-judged investments, and after three years ended up deeper in debt than he had been before. During these three years his activities seem to have progressed from the merely 'fast' to the barely legal, and in all probability to the downright criminal. I might mention, by the way, that he has been in the habit of acting under various aliases, a habit which did not make it easy to trace the details of his illustrious career. Much of my information on Harfield *fils* came through the kind offices of Lestrade, for Rupert Harfield has been known to the police for some years, though they have never had enough evidence to arrest him. Rather more than a year ago he lost the handsome house in which he had lived in splendour; it was mortgaged to the hilt, and finally the bailiffs threw him out. For a few months he lived in a succession of cheap rented rooms, usually fleeing at night owing rent, until he conceived the brilliant notion of moving in with his sister at her house in Belford Crescent.

"So much for Mr Rupert Harfield. I also managed to identify the doctor who visits Miss Matilda Harfield so assiduously. He is an old associate of Mr Rupert, and like him is known to the police without ever having been formally detained. He is known as Doctor Tobias Marshall. He completed but a single year of medical studies, and as far as I could find out, has no more right to style himself 'doctor' than I."

"What medicines had he prescribed for Miss Harfield?" I asked.

'I can show you," answered Holmes as he began rooting about among the retorts and dishes and papers that littered the table. "These are what I managed to take from Miss Harfield's room. Various vegetable alkalis; most of them powerful sedatives, but some stimulants too. Chloral hydrate here, and bromide – well, see for yourself."

I examined the labels. "I don't like the look of this, Holmes. All these medicines can be highly poisonous at the wrong dosage. Atropine – it can cause madness, as you know. Strychnine here – very similar – and yet no dose is given on either bottle. This is most irregular and disturbing. And what is the fellow's line of treatment? Why does he prescribe powerful sedatives and powerful stimulants for the same case?"

"Those were my thoughts precisely, Watson, when I looked at the medicines last week. This business begins to look very dark, would you not agree?"

"I would indeed. Do you suspect that he is deliberately making the lady ill? Is he poisoning her?" All my professional honour as a physician revolted at the thought. "That is a foul betrayal of trust, Holmes. It is unpardonable."

"I am not confident that there is any deliberate attack on the lady's life, though that is certainly a possibility. I am inclined to think that the attack is on her reason."

"You may well be right," I agreed. "Frenzy, delirium, loss of memory are all likely effects of the drugs here."

Holmes sat awhile in silence. He walked over to the window and opening a shutter, stared out at the night sky and the city beneath it. "What am I to do, Watson?" he asked. "The situation has changed. This case seemed merely curious at first, with Miss Davies bringing her intriguing tale of impossible events, but it has led us to a dangerous, cruel plot against an innocent woman. It is a serious and urgent matter now."

"My dear fellow," I answered, "there is surely no question about what you should do. You must go to the police."

"So that they may arrest Harfield?"

"Of course."

"On what charge?"

"He is trying to undermine Miss Harfield's health, to break her, body and mind."

"I am not aware that that is a criminal offence. An assault, perhaps? I am not sure. And even if there is a charge, what is the evidence? That another medical man has his doubts about the wisdom of the treatment being given."

"Well, yes, it sounds weak, I grant you, but there is also the matter of the piano-roll, and the voice down the chimney."

"A nervous maid thinks she heard a voice in her room, a private detective found a cigar-end on the roof, and a man plays piano-rolls on his piano. This is not evidence, Watson. All these poisonous medicines – every one of them is a recognised medicine, is it not, prescribed by hundreds of doctors? Any half-competent lawyer would laugh all our 'evidence' out of court."

"So you do not think the police would be prepared to arrest Harfield and charge him?"

"I do not."

"Wait a moment, Holmes. What about Miss Harfield? If she were to testify, surely a conviction would be likely."

"Ah, there is the problem in a nutshell. In her present state of mind she cannot possibly testify. She is forgetful, confused, probably delirious, deluded, and frightened. A worse witness cannot be imagined."

"But after a few weeks of care -"

"Indeed, after that, perhaps her brother could be arrested. And when might she be able to get those weeks of care, and be well enough to testify? Only after the arrest of her brother."

The truth was borne in upon on me; Miss Harfield was trapped. It was not so easy to see a way out. It was late, and I was tired, but I had little inclination to go to bed. I lit a cigarette and turned the problem over in my mind, but try though I might, I could find no solution. "Can anything be done?" I asked. "Can more evidence be collected, perhaps? I should be glad to give what help I can."

Holmes sat with his eyes closed. Were it not for the nervous drumming of his finger-tips on the arm of his chair, I might have thought he slept. "Suppose we try to gain more evidence, and in some way alert Harfield's suspicions," he said in a quiet voice, as if he were talking to himself. "What then? He might decamp with his sister. I have no doubt that in her present state he can get money out of her easily enough. We might lose track of him, and we would have made matters worse for her." After a long pause he continued. "On the other hand, what if I confront him? In that case, he can hardly continue his activities against his sister. Seeing himself discovered, and surrounded by the forces, official and unofficial, of the law, he will desist from his plot against her, and will probably flee the house. His sister will be saved, but he will escape justice."

"Are you sure you can scare him off?" I asked. "You were not sanguine a few minutes ago about the case against him."

"I was not sanguine about convincing a jury. I am a good deal more sanguine about convincing Harfield that he would not be well advised to continue his schemes under the eyes of Sherlock Holmes and the Metropolitan Police."

"Then to my mind there is no question as to what you should do. An innocent lady is in grave danger. You must save her, Holmes. If Harfield escapes, so be it. Will you stand by and watch her life destroyed in order that you may bring the destroyer to justice?"

"Ah, Watson, my one-man British jury! You are quite right, of course. Thank you; the issue is decided. I shall decide how to go about it tomorrow. For now, I bid you good-night."

It was two days later. Noon in Belford Crescent was the time and place Holmes had set for his meeting with

Harfield. Having spent the morning at the practice I returned at midday to Baker Street, whence we set off for Belford Crescent. "By the way, Watson," said Holmes, as we sat together in the cab, "my suggestion to Harfield that he receive us in his house was couched in terms which may lead him to suppose that the police are watching him. There is no need to disabuse him of his mistake." As our cab rattled past Regent's Park towards Kentish Town Holmes glanced keenly out at the world that flashed past; his eyes took on the alert glare of the predator. "Oh, another thing," he said. "You will be pleased to hear that we shall be joined by the mysterious organ-grinder, so-called."

"I shall be very interested to see him, at last," I replied, "but how do you know he will be there?"

"Because I sent him a note purporting to come from friend Harfield."

We left our cab at the western end of Belford Crescent and walked down. It was much as I had pictured it to be: a respectable little street, its terraced houses built in the stilted manner of the last century, their windows curtained and doorsteps scrubbed. As we made our way along the curve of the street we passed nobody; none of the traffic, wheeled and pedestrian, that thronged the busy high street we had just left had found its way down this little backwater. It was not difficult to see how the appearance of unaccountable strangers would cause such consternation here.

When we reached the Harfield house, Holmes strode up the steps and rapped on the door. It was opened by the maid Aggie. If she had any suspicion that Holmes was the delivery man whom she had admitted at the tradesmans' entrance a few days before, she did not show it. As we walked in, Holmes warned her in a low voice that two more gentlemen would be coming soon to join us and her master. "Yes sir," she said, and showed us into the parlour. There at the fireplace stood a tall man, pink in the face, a lock of fine tow hair falling over his brow. His elbow rested upon the mantelpiece as he looked coolly down at us from beneath his fair lashes. There was no doubt that we were in the presence of Mr Rupert Harfield. He took the cigar from his mouth and exhaled a cloud of blue smoke.

"I am a busy man, Mr Holmes, very busy. I trust that this conference is necessary."

"Not in the least, Mr Harfield," was Holmes's calm reply. "There is no necessity at all for my involvement. If you wish it the police will be very willing to pursue the matter instead. I am sorry to have troubled you; good day." With these words Holmes turned on his heel and made towards the door. I was about to follow him when Harfield called us back, with as good a show of bluster as he could manage. "Come now, you fellows! Now you're here, you might as well stay, both of you. I don't know what you want of me, or why you talk about the police, but I'll hear what you have to say."

Holmes replaced his hat and cane on the table. "That is very wise of you," said he in his most feline manner. "I assured my colleague here not an hour ago that you would listen to reason, did I not, Watson?"

At this moment the doorbell sounded, at which Harfield started visibly. "Don't be nervous, Mr Harfield," said Holmes. "I took the liberty of inviting your friends the Arrighelli brothers to our little meeting. This must be they." We heard Aggie open the door, and in a moment the brothers entered, to my unutterable astonishment. I seemed to be in the presence not of two men, but of one man and his reflection in a looking-glass. Evidently identical twins, they were stocky men in the late twenties, swarthy of skin and black of hair and eyes. In dress as well as person they were identical, down to the red flannel waistcoats with brass buttons of which I had heard so much. The pair frowned and flashed quick glances at me and Holmes, evidently puzzled by our presence. They nodded curtly to Harfield; their eyes seemed to ask what was going on, but they said not a word.

"Good afternoon, gentlemen. I am Mr Sherlock Holmes," said my friend, "and this is my colleague Dr Watson. Mr Rupert Harfield, of course, you know. It was I who left the note for you asking you to come here today. You will forgive my little subterfuge. We are here to discuss the events of the last month or so, events in which you played your part. Now you are here, let us proceed." He turned to Harfield. "I shall outline what took place. Pray correct any inaccuracies.

"It all started a month ago when you, Mr Harfield, stored some stolen goods in this house. Unfortunately for you, your sister saw them. She confronted you and insisted that the goods be removed. You arranged for them to be taken away at night, in secret. But you still had quite a problem, did you not? Suppose she told her friends, or worse, went to the police? How could you be sure that would never happen? You thought of your sister's mild, perhaps timid disposition, and you saw a way of playing on this weakness; you decided to make her mistrust herself, to doubt the evidence of her own senses; you would make it appear to herself and others that she was a wholly unreliable witness. To this end you devised a number of cunning tricks designed to undermine what little self-assurance she possessed." Holmes counted them off on his fingers as he spoke. "Firstly, when you knew your sister to be in her room you climbed out on to the roof, onto the chimney-stack and spoke vile phrases down the chimney that served her fireplace, so that she would believe herself to be hearing imaginary voices."

The brothers, still frowning as they listened, muttered to each other in Italian, with an occasional angry gesture.

"Then there was the mysterious piano music. You had some rolls made of imperfect piano-playing, complete with false notes and corrected mistakes. Exactly how did you make use of them, I wonder? Did you perhaps deny to Miss Harfield that you heard anything while the piano was playing? Perhaps you even showed her the empty room, with noone at the piano. The poor lady must have been quite convinced that she was losing her reason.

"Another little scheme involved the brothers Arrighelli here. You persuaded them to appear, identically dressed, in different parts of the crescent. I note that the days on which they appeared were the days on which your sister ventured out for a short constitutional. One of the brothers would be stationed outside your house – your sister's house, I should say – where she could not fail to see him, and the other would be waiting round the corner, evidently a creature with supernatural powers of locomotion. What could she think, but that she was seeing things as well as hearing them?"

"I don't know what the devil you're talking about," snarled Harfield.

"This was all a joke, he tells us," exclaimed one of the brothers.

"He tells us, it will be funny," continued the other. "His

157

sister she will think it very funny," the fellow shouted, spitting out the words and glaring at Harfield. "We don't know nothing about this bad thing, he don't tell us nothing."

Harfield had quite lost his blustering poise, despite his pretence of denial. He stood there, a crumpled figure against the mantelpiece as Holmes continued his inexorable account of events.

"Now we come to the medical treatment you arranged for Miss Harfield. Medical treatment, did I say? I had rather call it a systematic derangement of the senses, forced upon an innocent woman against her will or without her knowledge. Bromide, chloral, strychnia, atropine in unspecified quantities – these have all been prescribed for your sister. Or have I made a mistake? Shall we go upstairs and check on the medicines there?"

"You can do as you damned well please," muttered Harfield.

"When, I wonder," continued Holmes, "did the idea of having her pronounced insane come to you? Should she be committed to an insane asylum, you as her next of kin would get your hands on her house and her money. What had begun as a defence against her telling what she knew grew into a solution to your financial problems. Perhaps you hoped that the drugs with which you plied her would result in her death."

"I never did!" cried Harfield from the floor. "That's a damned lie."

"Indeed? I shall take your word for it – although now you have spoken out in denial of that charge, I think we can safely take your silence concerning the other charges as an admission of guilt."

Throughout my friend's exposition the brothers'

muttering had been rising in a crescendo of what sounded like oaths. Suddenly one of them dashed forward; in an instant he was upon Harfield, and with a terrific blow sent him crashing into the fireplace. As I lunged forward and pulled him back by his arm the other twin moved forward, fists clenched. Harfield cowered on the floor amid the scattered poker and fire-tongs, wiping blood from his mouth and looking up in terror at the brothers.

"Enough now, you two!" cried Holmes. "The police will be arriving soon."

Mention of the police was enough for the pair. A quick glance flashed between them; they both twisted round and spat on their fallen foe, and in an instant rushed past us. I moved to stop them, but Holmes held up his hand to stay me.

"Let them go, Watson, let them go." We heard the front door open, and a moment later, through the window, I saw them running down the street. "I have no great quarrel with the Arrighelli brothers. It's pretty clear they had no idea what harm their little deception was designed to inflict. No, this is the fellow I was after," said my friend, indicating the supine figure of Harfield. "Might I suggest, Watson, that you go upstairs and remove the battery of medicines from Miss Harfield's room? We may hold them in safekeeping for the police. Let us hope that the damage is not permanent, and that the unfortunate lady's condition will improve once Mr Rupert Harfield has been removed from her home and her life."

The Case of the Standing Wheat

I returned one evening to the Baker Street flat I shared
with Sherlock Holmes to find that my fellow-lodger was
not alone; a furtive-looking little man was perched on the
edge of the easy-chair, turning his hat round and round
in his hands. He glanced up at me sharply as I entered.

"Ah, Watson!" exclaimed Holmes. "Your masterly
sense of timing has not deserted you. Inspector Lestrade
here is about to tell me of a case that has been causing the
force some concern."

"It is not my own case, you know," said the inspector.
"It's down in Sussex, and the local constabulary is in
charge. Perhaps you have heard about it; Lowe farm, near
Birley, is the place, and the man held is the farmer, name
of Queeny."

"I read a report in this morning's paper, yes," I
answered, settling into a chair.

"I wonder that you take an interest in it, Lestrade, if
you are not handling the matter," intervened Holmes. "I
suppose you have not enough work of your own on hand."

This remark elicited a snort of outrage from the
inspector. "Believe me, Mr Holmes, I have enough and
more on my plate, I can assure you of that. No, that's not

it, but I'll tell you what my interest in the case is. The enquiry is in the hands of the local man, Chief Inspector Ellery, and Ellery is an old friend of mine. We trained together, and were promoted to inspector in the same year. There are a couple of oddities about this Lowe Farm case that Ellery couldn't fathom, and last night he came up to see me about it. Quite informal, mind you; he doesn't want to see the Yard called in. It would hurt his professional pride, you see. Of course, he knows of you, Mr Holmes, and he knows you have worked with me a few times. And he knows that when you have been involved in a case, you haven't always insisted on taking the credit. Well, if you were able to give him any help, I should say that he'd be very grateful, though he's too proud a man to ask. I should be grateful too; there's not a finer man in the force than Jack Ellery, and I don't want to see him fail."

"So your old comrade Ellery consulted with you," said Holmes, "and you in turn consult with me. I think I had better hear what has provoked this flurry of consultation." He pushed the cigarette-box towards our visitor. "Take one of these, make yourself comfortable in the easy-chair, and tell us what you know about the death at Lowe Farm."

The inspector gathered his thoughts for a few moments, frowning and turning his bowler hat round and round in his hands.

"There's little enough to tell," he began, "and I'm not sure old Jack Ellery isn't making a mountain out of a molehill. Be that as it may, the facts of the matter are these:

"Yesterday, at about seven in the morning, the farm-hand at Lowe comes from the upper fields, where he has been mending a gate. He goes down to the barn, which lies by the lower field. The lower field is a wheat-field, not yet harvested. He notices a number of crows in one corner. So he goes into the wheat to scare them off, and up they rise in a great flock and he sees what they have been feeding on. It's the body of a man, lying in the wheat. Straight away the lad runs over to the house to fetch his master, John Queeny. He finds Queeny at the house all right, but he's the worse for drink, and refuses to move. When Fairbrother – that's the farm-hand – begs him to come, his employer flings a bottle at him and tells him to go to the devil."

"What an extraordinary response!" I exclaimed.

"Not so extraordinary as you might think, Dr Watson," replied the inspector. "Not for this man Queeny, at any rate. He is given to occasional fits of very hard drinking, they say, when he becomes surly, violent, and morose. These bouts of drunkenness last several days, during which time nobody goes near him. In the end he sleeps it off and emerges, grim-faced and foul-tempered, to work again on the farm.

"Well, young Billy Fairbrother finds himself in a quandary. His master won't come, and there's no-one else he can turn to, for he's the only hand on the farm, and Queeny lives alone without a housekeeper or servant. So Fairbrother has no choice but to go to the village himself and alert the constable. He is obliged to walk, for Queeny does not keep a horse. He sets off, and the village lying some four miles distant, it isn't much before noon that he returns to the farm, accompanied by the village constable. As soon as they arrive the constable, having made a brief inspection of the scene, instructs Fairbrother to guard the body, while he himself makes sure that Queeny doesn't leave the house. And so they remain for an hour or so until my friend Ellery comes on the scene, with two constables and surgeon.

"The surgeon carries out a preliminary examination of the body, and then has the constables remove it, and in the meantime Ellery carefully checks the ground where the body lies. The greatest care was taken not to disturb the ground, Mr Holmes," added the inspector, with a glance towards my friend.

"Of course," answered Holmes. "Pray continue."

"Well, the surgeon confirms what has been obvious enough already, that the dead man has suffered the most severe injuries, including a broken neck, a broken leg, broken ribs, severe bruising and some lacerations. Death, which must have followed the injuries immediately, occurred between ten and seven hours before the examination - in other words between three o'clock at night and six in the morning. Nothing was found that might identify him."

Holmes had risen and walked over to the window, where he stood gazing out as though quite uninterested in the inspector's tale. Without taking his eyes from the clouds that drifted across the sky he interrupted the policeman:

"Nothing at all?"

"Not a thing."

"No wallet? No name in his hat? No card? No initials on his watch?"

"Nothing, Mr Holmes. All I can tell you is this, that he was a man in early middle age, in good health, of good height, slender frame, and well enough dressed."

"I see. So the dead man remains unidentified?"

"That is so."

"Pray continue."

"Now, the farmer Queeny - or perhaps I should say the small-holder, for his place is not above thirty acres - John Queeny, I say, lives alone on his land. His wife is dead and, as I said, he has no servant or housekeeper. His only help in working his farm is this lad Fairbrother, who lives in the neighbouring farmstead with his parents and walks across to Queeny's every day. In the summer months Fairbrother arrives there at dawn and leaves at dusk; so he did yesterday morning."

"Whose word do you have for that?"

"Fairbrother's own. He made a full statement to Inspector Ellery."

"Not Queeny's?"

"Queeny has not made a statement."

Holmes nodded and waved the inspector to continue.

"There's not much doubt about who did it, Mr Holmes. For one thing, only a great lumbering ox of a man like Queeny could have inflicted the injuries we saw. Further, he has a most foul reputation among his neighbours as a violent, ill-tempered bully. No man, woman or child is safe when he is in drink. They say that his cruel use of his wife hastened her early death, and he has twice been in trouble with the authorities over assaulting his hired men. Fairbrother is a very different type of person - a simple young man, he is, they say, a gentle soul. Besides which, he is half the size of Queeny - I don't say he is a weakling, but he lacks the strength to inflict the terrible injuries that the stranger suffered. It all points one way, gentlemen, and accordingly Queeny is now under arrest on suspicion of murder."

"I see. Well, as the local police seem to have the matter well in hand, I am not quite clear how I can help," commented Holmes.

"I'm inclined to agree with you there, Mr Holmes. Ellery has his man under close arrest, and the process of the law can take its course. What more does he need to do? But you see, Ellery is a stickler for detail, and there are one or two details that he can't quite explain to his satisfaction. He worries about them - worries too much, to my way of thinking. You can't always expect to understand every little thing about a case. Life doesn't work out that way and no more does police work. But he doesn't see it like that. I have no doubt, Mr Holmes, that if you could be prevailed upon to help him he would be a deal happier."

"Then you had better tell me about these details that so trouble your friend Inspector Ellery."

"Well, firstly, the identity of the dead man. We can't find out who he is - or was, should I say. None of the local men is missing. That's one thing. Next, how did he get there? No tracks to where he lay, and no sign of what must surely have been a most terrible struggle. We don't have a weapon, either. It must have been something akin to a sledgehammer that delivered those blows, but nothing has been found."

"Considerable difficulties, are they not? Do you have any theory to explain them?"

" 'Theory?' " The inspector leaned forward in his chair. "I don't know about theories, Mr Holmes," he answered, "but I can make a plain guess. There are a few gangs of labourers travelling the area, looking for harvest work. Gipsies, some of them. They visit all the local farms, offering themselves for hire. Now, suppose Queeny is drinking at his place with one of those fellows, and they fall out. The labourer storms out; the farmer follows in a rage, and fells him. He carries the body away from the house to the field where he pitches it into the corn, leaving as few tracks as possible."

Holmes was still standing at the window, watching the evening clouds scudding high overhead. After a long silence he turned to us. "There is something about this case that arouses my curiosity. How are you fixed for tomorrow, Watson? Could you leave your practice for the day?"

"Certainly. My neighbour will take my place. I have done as much for him several times recently."

"Good man! That settles it. We shall go down to Birley, in Sussex, tomorrow."

Lestrade, never at ease for long in a chair, leapt to his feet. "I'll leave this copy of the surgeon's summary for you," he said, tapping the sheaf of papers he had brought with him. "I'm pleased you'll be helping my friend Ellery, Mr Holmes, very pleased. I'll admit it's a puzzler in some respects, this case. But there's only one man who could have done this murder, and that man is Queeny. He'll swing for this, I'll wager, and when he does, no-one will mourn his passing."

With these prophetic words the inspector gave us goodnight, and left.

Holmes and I took an early train the next morning to Birley. We were met at the station by a constable and driven to the police station, where we were ushered into a side room to wait for Ellery. After a few minutes the door opened and in burst a splendid figure of a man, tall and broad-chested, with a bold stride that befitted the veldt better than the little fields of Surrey. He introduced himself as inspector Ellery; and as he shook my hand with a firm grip and looked me straight in the eye, I could not help thinking wryly that this fine specimen of English manhood was as different from the dark, furtive little Lestrade as it was possible for a fellow to be. Ellery thanked us for coming, and immediately got down to the matter in hand. The suspect Queeny was in the cell below, he told us, and the body of the man he was charged with murdering was also in the station; it was agreed that Holmes should interview Queeny, then examine the body, and finally pay a visit to Lowe Farm, Queeny's smallholding where the body had been found. Ellery took us down to the cell, looked through the peep-hole, and unlocked the door. The three of us entered.

In the course of my association with Sherlock Holmes I have visited a number of suspects in police custody. It is a situation in which few men are seen to advantage, and Queeny cut as poor a figure as any. We found him slumped in the corner of his cell, glaring listlessy up at us as we entered. His huge bulk was more pathetic than menacing, like that of the caged bear whose claws and teeth are drawn. He sullenly denied having murdered the man; indeed, he was adamant that he had been alone all that night, and had not seen a soul until the hired man Fairbrother had burst in on him the next morning. On this simple point he was obstinate; further questioning brought nothing but oaths or grunts. After a few minutes even these unhelpful responses dried up and were replaced by a morose silence. "Friend Queeny was not very communicative, was he?" Holmes cheerfully remarked as we left the cell. "Let us hope the dead man will tell us more than the living one."

The body was laid out under a sheet in an upstairs room, and beside it, on a bench, were laid out the dead man's clothes and the contents of his pockets. Holmes looked through them one by one. "A remarkably sturdy coat and waist-coat for the summer months," he muttered. "Perhaps he knew that he was to be abroad in the small hours. No maker's name. Stout canvas boots . . . with soles of gutta-percha. No hat." He turned to the smaller basket. "Now, let us see what he carried in his pockets. A handkerchief; some coins; a clasp-knife: what do you make of the knife, Inspector?" he asked.

The inspector took the knife in his hand. "Well, I should say it was a pocket-knife of ordinary design, by no means new," he answered, handing it back.

"Yes, it is well-worn," agreed Holmes, "and also well-preserved. See how readily it opens; probably because -" he lifted it to his nostrils - "yes, a faint smell of gun-oil. He cleaned it, I see, as well as oiling it. Sharpened it recently, too - do you see the shine on the edge where it was honed?" he asked, turning the blade to catch the light. "And sharpened it often: see how the blade is worn hollow. What else do we have? Ah, his fob-watch! This is a fine time-piece - not quite a marine chronometer, I suppose - a deck-watch, perhaps. Well-tended, like his knife, but it isn't going. It gives four minutes after three o'clock." He put the watch to his ear. "Perhaps it needs winding . . . no, it is broken. That is indicative. Nothing else – no pocket-book, for example?" he asked himself, looking through the basket. "No. Then let us turn to the body itself."

The orderly pulled back the sheet to reveal the body. Holmes examined it in silence for some ten minutes before replacing the sheet and turning to us. "Very much as the doctor reported, of course. Not much new to learn here, I think. Let us move on to Queeny's place. I should like to see where the body was found." We returned to the station to pick up a dog-cart.

"Tell me, Mr Holmes, did our doctor miss anything in his report? Have you learnt anything new about the dead man?" Ellery asked as we jolted along the lanes on our way to Queeny's farm.

"No, no," came the answer. "Only the hands. Did you not notice? The palms were calloused."

"I had not noticed the palms of the hands, no. A labouring man, do you think?"

"I think not. His accoutrements do not suggest it, and his hands were well enough manicured. No case under the nails, for instance."

Ellery looked puzzled, until his eyes lit on his own hands holding the reins. "A riding man!" he exclaimed.

Holmes, however, seemed to have lost interest in this line of enquiry, and became absorbed in the countryside through which we were passing. It was a bright day, and the wheat harvest was in spate. In some of the fields we passed, gangs of harvest-men were busy in the sun; some fields were empty, already harvested, and reduced to bare stubble; in others, the ripe wheat still stood, rippling in the breeze.

After some twenty minutes of this pleasant journey a sign saying LOWE FARM came into view. There we turned into a narrow, overgrown track, and as we headed up to the farmhouse we passed the wheat-field where the body had been found. Holmes desired to be let down immediately, and down we all jumped. The field, one of those as yet unharvested, was surrounded on three sides by a low, scrubby hedge, the fourth side being edged by a ditch. In the corner by which we entered grew two old elms, beyond whose spread began the wheat. A constable standing in the shade of the trees saluted our arrival. He was, Ellery explained, guarding the spot where the body had lain, about thirty yards beyond the trees. Holmes approached the spot with as much circumspection as if the body were still there, cautiously examining the damaged wheat, often dropping to his knees to peer at the ground with his magnifying lens, sometimes taking out his tape-measure, although to measure what, I could not see. Whatever the measurements were, he jotted them down in his note-book, while Ellery, his constable and I waited patiently under the trees, observing this procedure with some curiosity. If the two policemen were a little surprised by the minute care with which Holmes carried out his investigations, they were a good deal more surprised when he emerged from the wheat and knelt at their feet to examine their own footprints.

"Lord, Mr Holmes," exclaimed Ellery with good humour, "I trust we are not suspects?"

"I need to know who went where, Inspector. I shall not be able to identify the footmarks of the murderer or his victim, if I cannot distinguish their tread from yours. Now, the labourer Fairbrother: he is a smallish fellow with a spring in his step?"

The inspector's eyebrows shot up. "Quite right, Mr Holmes! You have him in one."

Holmes nodded and looked about him. He wandered slowly about under the trees, looking in all directions: he peered over to the far corners of the field, and beyond them, I thought, towards the distant rolling hills of the South Downs. He then turned his gaze inland towards Surrey, whence we had come, and then eastwards towards the Romney Marshes. He looked up; the uppermost branches of the trees danced lightly over our heads, and far above a few hazy clouds were scudding across the sky. For what seemed many minutes my friend stood thus absorbed in his surroundings. Had I not known him better, I should perhaps have thought him rapt in some bucolic reverie, but my long acquaintance with him suggested otherwise. I was sure that his dreamy, abstracted mien reflected his musings not on the beauties of the Sussex countryside, but on the violent death that had disgraced them. Suddenly, as was his way, he snapped out of his dreamy speculations and was again his masterful self, taut with nervous vigour.

"Inspector Ellery, I should like a word with young Fairbrother; and also the use of a pair of field-glasses."

"There is a pocket-telescope at the cottage, sir, if that will serve," –Holmes nodded his assent– "and Fairbrother has been told to remain close at hand, at his family's place, just over the way. I shall send for him. The cottage is this way, gentlemen."

The cottage was a low, ill-favoured building. The constable standing on guard by the door was duly sent on his mission to fetch Fairbrother, and we three went in, all of us being obliged to lower our heads as we entered. Ellery and I sat down at the deal table, while Holmes ferretted about for anything that could give him information. He examined and measured two pairs of boots, peered into drawers and cupboards, read papers, and sniffed or tasted the contents of jars and bottles. Once satisfied that he had seen all that was to be seen downstairs, he continued his researches upstairs. For several minutes we heard his quick, light steps above our heads, and then he scurried down the stairs and out of the house, where he fell to examining the muddy grass and flags as he had examined the corner of the wheatfield. Eventually he pocketed his measure, lens and note-book, and joined us at the table. Ellery was eager to know, naturally, if he had he had as yet any idea as to what had happened, but he was to be disappointed, for before Holmes had time to answer him, the constable returned with the farm-hand Fairbrother.

The young labourer stood before us, his hair the colour of straw, his skin burnt to a darker shade. He shifted his weight from one foot to another and picked at the straw hat in his hands.

"This is Mr Holmes, the detective," said Ellery. "He would like to ask you a few questions."

Holmes took a cigarette from his case and lit it. "Billy," said he, "I want you to tell me what happened yesterday morning."

"When I got here, which it had not been daylight long, I went to the cottage first of all - "

"One moment," interrupted Holmes. "Before you reached the cottage, as you walked to Queeny's place, did you see anything unusual? Did you see someone on Queeny's land, for instance? Did you see someone leaving it?"

"I didn't see no-one, sir, no, but that don't mean they weren't there."

"Surely you would have seen anyone who was there?"

"Not yesterday morning, sir. There was a mist that morning. When I looked over to Queeny's place all I could see was clouds."

"I see. How long did the mist last?"

"It was clear and bright by 7 o'clock, sir. Sea-mists don't last long."

"It came in off the sea, you think?"

"Oh yes, sir, I reckon so. That was a fierce wind, too,

the night before last. An east wind, blowing in off the German Ocean and bringing a deal of the ocean with it."

"Tell us what happened once you reached the farm."

Billy Fairbrother continued his story of the morning's events. I shall not weary the reader with all the details again, for the labourer's account agreed in every respect with that of Lestrade given at the beginning of this record. One detail of Lestrade's account in particular Fairbrother confirmed categorically, namely, that the body when he found it lay in untouched, standing wheat. He could suggest no answer to Holmes's question as to how the body might have got there, but was none the less insistent that there were no trodden-down stalks; the body had lay in the midst of virgin wheat.

"It's a poser," said Ellery, shaking his head, after the labourer had left us. "I've puzzled over it, Mr Holmes, again and again, but I can't fathom it at all. What do you make of it?"

"I make nothing of it as yet, Inspector."

At these words Ellery's face fell. "Well, if it's got England's premier consulting detective flummoxed," he said, "I don't know what a country policeman can do." We knew in what high regard the inspector regarded Holmes; it was natural that he should be sadly disenchanted to find that his idol had feet of clay.

"Do you not have enough information, Mr Holmes?" asked Ellery. "We thought that there might be an answer to this case somewhere here, some vital clue that we had missed." He shrugged his broad shoulders. "We set our hopes too high, it seems. I guess we have overlooked nothing, after all. Perhaps we will never know just what happened last night."

"Perhaps so," answered Holmes. "After all, success in

these matters cannot be commanded, inspector, as you know. But to answer your question, I think that I do have enough information. In any event, no further information is likely to come to light now; we have garnered all we can. No, the problem now is not to gather more facts; it is to put together the facts we have and make sense of them. And that, gentlemen, requires uninterrupted thought."

So saying, he rose to his feet and, without another word to either of us, went out of the cottage into the yard and crossed to a dilapidated outhouse. There he climbed into the back of a broken cart, settled himself comfortably, and lit his pipe. Soon puffs of smoke were drifting up from his motionless figure as if in answer to the clouds drifting across the sky. The inspector and I exchanged a few words as we awaited Holmes' return, but when after a good many minutes my friend showed no sign of returning, the inspector decided to 'cut his losses', as he phrased it to me, and went over to the wheatfield to confer with his constable. I whiled away the time by strolling around Queeny's smallholding.

On my return I found Holmes exactly as I had left him, sprawled in the back of the cart. A frown of concentration on his brow told me that the mystery remained unsolved. "An *impasse*, Watson. I cannot make headway. The question is, how did the body get into the field without the wheat being disturbed? Until that question is answered, everything else is mere speculation. That one circumstance is the key to the understanding of this case, would you not agree?" He frowned again and drew on his pipe. "How many times have I said that it is the bizarre cases that can be understood, and the commonplace ones that can have any number of solutions? Well, this case seems to be the exception to my rule. It looks as if friend

Ellery is going to be disappointed," he said with a shrug of resignation, leaning back against the boards. "I cannot delay my return to London any longer. The train leaving at half-past four this afternoon is the latest I can take if I am to keep my appointment with the Foreign Secretary. I had better have a word with Ellery, and then we shall be on our way back."

Holmes clambered out of the cart and brushed the dust and straw from his coat. We walked to the wheatfield, where we found Ellery still in conservation with his constable. The inspector strode up to us as we approached him. "Well, Mr Holmes, have you come to an opinion?"

"I'm sorry to tell you, inspector, that I have not. I wish that I could spend more time looking into your very interesting case, but, alas, I cannot."

The inspector tried to hide his disappointment. "At least," he said, "it is some consolation to know that where I failed, the great Sherlock Holmes failed too."

We drove with him in silence to the station, where we shook hands and parted. Holmes and I sat on the platform bench to wait for the train. Above us a few white clouds moved slowly in the blue sky, while around us floated thistledown, shining in the sunlight. To the constant murmuring of the doves was added an occasional distant shout from the labourers in the fields. It was indeed a perfect summer's day; more the pity, I thought, that Holmes' failure soured its sweetness for us. As this rueful reflection crossed my mind, I suddenly felt my companion stiffen next to me. In an instant he leapt to his feet and smote his brow with the flat of his hand. "How slow I have been!" he exclaimed. "The thistledown, Watson! The thistledown!"

"Yes, I see some thistledown," I answered, unable to share his sudden enthusiasm. "Perhaps you could tell me what bearing a few whisps – "

Before I could finish my question Holmes was running down the platform. He hammered on the station-master's door and without waiting for a reply flung it open and rushed in. I followed him and looked in at the door to see an open-mouthed railwayman handing him a telephone. Holmes grasped the instrument and demanded the police station.

"This is Sherlock Holmes. I wish to speak to Inspector Ellery. No? Then please to give him this message. You have a pencil and paper? My compliments to the inspector, and I suggest that he search for a hot-air balloon station lying on a line east-north-east from here at a distance of at least 20 miles. That is all."

He passed the apparatus back to the open-mouthed official. "Thank you. Is that the London train I hear coming in?"

Too astonished to speak, the man nodded his assent.

"Come then, Watson!" Holmes turned on his heel, and brushed past me. I followed him out, and we climbed aboard the train.

As we jolted back to London Holmes lay back in his seat and gazed out at the fields and hamlets of Sussex rolling past. "Not my finest moment, Watson. How can I have been so slow? After all, the case was fundamentally a simple one. It hinged upon a single question; how did the body arrive in an untouched cornfield? Ellery was quite right not to ignore that question. It was the key to the whole mystery. You noticed, I dare say, that I was careful to confirm that the wheat had indeed been undisturbed, and that the trampling we saw had been done only by Fairbrother and the police, and not by Queeny, the dead man, or anybody else. The dead man's hands and belongings suggested a sea-faring background, but that simply added to the mystery; why would a sailor, of all people, end up dead in a Sussex corn-field fifteen miles from the coast? Then there was the matter of the weather; there had been a wind and a fog during the night. Was that connected somehow with the man's death? Possibly, but I could not see how. I puzzled over it for hours, trying in vain to connect these different threads. It was only once I had given up the case as a bad job that those whisps of thistledown carried by the breeze told me the truth. The dead man had been carried by the wind himself, in a balloon, and fallen from it. That is why there were no tracks leading to his body, and why he suffered such crushing injuries."

"But that hardly explains – ah, but it does!" I exclaimed as the truth dawned on me. "The shoes, the watch – what seemed to be sailor's gear was really balloonist's gear."

"Precisely."

"A brilliant insight, Holmes! The whole mystery clears away like morning mist. But how did you know what instructions to give on the position of the balloonist's station? I can't follow you there, I'm afraid."

"Simple enough, Watson. The wind that blew in the fog and the balloon was an East-north-easterly. So the ballon had come from that direction. How far in that direction I am uncertain, but somewhere roughly along that line must lie the station from which the balloon set out.

"Quite the *deus ex machina*, is it not? But you may have been somewhat hasty in your congratulations,

Watson. Perhaps my explanation does have something in the way of ingenuity, but it is, after all, a speculation only. The most brilliant theory is of little value if it has not the merit of truth. What if no hot-air ballon station is to be found? What then? I shall have made a thorough-going fool of myself, and inspector Ellery's estimation of me will fall even lower than it is at present. I could wish that I had the time to search for the balloon station myself, but alas! the matter is out of my hands. I dared not risk missing this train; foreign secretaries do not like to be kept waiting. I can only hope that my surmise will prove correct, after all, and that my reputation, such as it is, will be spared from ridicule."

Thus ended my friend's involvement in the strange case of the body in the wheatfield. Like it or no, he was obliged by promises given and by his sense of public duty to leave the final details of this rural mystery to the local police, and to plunge himself instead into an autumn of extraordinary activity, some of which I have chronicled elsewhere. The story itself, however, did not end quite there. A week after Holmes and I had left the village of Birley the following paragraph appeared in the *Daily Telegraph*:

DEATH IN THE SEA FOG.
EXPERIENCED BALLOONIST IN FATAL ACCIDENT.

Triumph of Local Constabulary.

We can reveal the identity of the hitherto unknown man whose body was found in mysterious circumstances in the

Sussex village of Birley, as reported in this journal two weeks ago. The dead man was Mr Warrington Maude, of Farrell, in Kent. Mr Maude, an engineer and and farmer, was well known locally as an enthusiastic and devoted balloonist. He was the owner of a ballooning station which he ran with his younger brother Alfred. The Maude brothers, who made many flights for the entertainment of passengers, were equally assiduous in carrying out scientific investigations in their balloons, and for some weeks, we are informed, the elder Mr Maude had been engaged in a series of flights as part of his research into Aetherial Drift. On the morning of his untimely death, Mr Warrington Maude set out on such a flight just after dawn, as had become his custom. The weather at that hour was calm, and Mr Maude, it must be supposed, effected a rapid and easy ascent. On that morning, however, as ill-luck would have it, a strong east-north-easterly wind sprang up within an hour of sunrise, carrying with it a thick bank of sea-fog. Fog, we are informed, is the balloonist's greatest enemy, as it is the mariner's, for deprived of the power of observation, he must perforce remain unaware of even the most imminent danger. Mr Maude was blown twenty miles, unable to know where he was or whither he was going, until the top branches of an unusually high tree in a Sussex small-holding caught the carriage of his balloon. Precipitated from it, he fell to his immediate death, leaving the balloon to continue its journey unmanned.

The astute reader may ask how the details given in the preceding paragraph came to be known, since the lamentable episode was unwitnessed. His answer lies in the keen detective power of Inspector Ellery, the officer in charge of the case. As was reported in these pages earlier, the small-holder on whose land the dead man was found, Mr John Queeny, was initially held on suspicion, but the enquiry, as it proceeded, revealed circumstances which mitigated strongly against Mr Queeny's guilt. The appearance of the body in the midst of undamaged wheat indicated that it had arrived from above; "an extraordinary conclusion," the inspector told your correspondent, "but the body could not have arrived by any other way; and when all other possibilities have been excluded, the remaining one, however improbable, must be the truth." The inspector's reasoning was vindicated, for a careful calculation of the wind's direction and strength guided the investigation to the Maude station in Farrell, where the sad truth was discovered.

Mr Warrington Maude, originally from Northallerton, was a well-known figure in local circles, and a respected contributor to several scientific and philosophical publications. He was a bachelor, and leaves as his closest kin his brother Alfred.

The Black Bull

'SHERLOCK HOLMES FAILS IN BANK THEFT,' ran the headline. I flung down the paper and picked up another. It told the same story:

'THEFT OF DIAMONDS FROM BANK VAULT
'Leading Detective foiled by Thieves

'A robbery was effected yesterday against the London branch of the Hanseatic bank. An unusually valuable consignment of diamonds, recently arrived from Amsterdam, was the target of this daring outrage, which succeeded despite the presence in the bank of both the police and the private detective Mr Sherlock Holmes. The official police and Mr Holmes, having been called in by the directors of the bank in response to intelligence received concerning a planned robbery, scrutinised the safe-box containing the diamonds as it entered the vault of the bank, and satisfied themselves that the contents were safely arrived: but in the afternoon, when the box was opened again, it was found to be empty. The directors have no idea how the theft was effected. Inspector Symons, who leads the police enquiry, assures us that although no explanation has been found to date, the crime is being investigated with the utmost zeal.

The press of the previous few days had been carrying similar reports of Holmes's activities. One paper told of a murder in Birmingham; a householder had been killed during the commission of a burglary, and Holmes had been called in by the murdered man's business partner to assist the police enquiry. At the time of publication, the article had claimed, no arrest had been made. Another report described an escape from Bedford gaol. The escape was no extraordinary matter, and received but a brief mention; its sole point of interest, for me at least, being the presence of Sherlock Holmes. He had visited the gaol to speak with a prisoner on that day, and it was during some confusion occasioned by this interview that another prisoner in the same wing had broken free.

What was I to make of these reports? For over a month I had seen neither hide nor hair of Holmes, nor even received so much as a note or telegram. Yet the length and breadth of the country he was busy investigating one crime after another, and, if these reports were to be believed, meeting with little success. I was quite at a loss to make sense of what was happening. The situation seemed as tangled and puzzling as any of Holmes's cases.

It had begun some five weeks earlier, when I had come down one morning to find Holmes already seated at the breakfast table, drinking coffee and reading the morning's paper, for all the world as if he were an ordinary professional man like myself, ready for a day's work at his office. I pointed out that his company at breakfast was a rare pleasure for me, and hoped that he had the time to take another cup of coffee with me.

He put down the paper and glanced up at the clock. "Yes, I have a few minutes to spare. My train leaves Victoria Station at fourteen minutes past eight. The cab is waiting downstairs."

"Victoria, you say – you have a case on the south coast?"

"On the Continent."

"I must congratulate you, Holmes. Your reputation knows no bounds. It must be an important matter that takes you so far afield."

"Several important matters, but you will forgive me if I go no further in satisfying your curiosity. I am enjoined to silence."

"My dear fellow, I quite understand. Do you know how long you will be engaged?"

"I do not. Even on the surface the business is complicated enough, and heaven knows how deep its roots go. To make matters yet more difficult, I must act in secrecy, for where the highest in this and other lands are concerned, one cannot create a stir that might alarm our people at home or warn our enemies abroad."

"Of course." I had taken the other place at table and begun to make inroads upon the kedgeree. "You know I take the keenest interest in your cases, Holmes, and I should dearly like know the outcome of these enquiries as they unfold, but as they are to be so discreet, I assume that I shall hardly be able to follow your progress in the newspapers."

"Not directly, no; but if during the next fortnight they carry no reports of the Foreign Secretary's resignation or an outbreak of hostilities in the Balkans, then you may take it that the first part of my commission has succeeded." He drained his cup and rose from the table. "I fancy I have already said more than I should; but I know," he added with a meaning glance, "that I can rely on your complete discretion. Where did I put my bag? Ah, there it is." He seized his travelling-bag, and with a breezy "Fare thee well, Watson!" bounded down the stairs.

Week followed week, bringing news neither of war in Eastern Europe, nor of the fall of her Majesty's Secretary for Foreign Affairs. I was not in the least disconcerted by my friend's continued absence, for years of sharing rooms with him had inured me to his unpredictable ways. I had every confidence that one evening I should come home to our Baker Street lodgings to find Holmes lying on the sofa in his dressing gown, greeting my entry with a casual wave as if we had last seen each other that morning. I expected no more warning of his return than that; but I was mistaken, for it fell out that I learned of his return, as I have just described, in the daily press.

So, discarded newspapers at my feet, I was brooding unhappily upon what I had read when my train of thought was interrupted by a sharp double rap. The door opened and round it appeared a face I recognised as that a Scotland Yard police officer who had been involved in several of Sherlock Holmes's cases.

"Inspector Lestrade, is it not?" I asked. "Come in, come

in. I take it that you have come to see Mr Holmes. If so, I'm afraid I must disappoint you."

"Good evening, Dr Watson. Yes, I understand from your landlady that he is still away from home. That is a pity; I should very much like to have a word with him."

"I have not seen him myself these last five weeks, inspector. Well, take a seat. You are welcome to a word with me, if I can help."

"If I do not intrude."

"Not at all. I dined some time ago and was merely reading the evening paper."

"So I see," he replied, glancing at the newspapers that lay around me. "You have been following Mr Holmes's latest escapades, I suppose."

"I have read a couple of reports about his work since he returned from the Continent, yes. I have no idea where he is now, though, or what he is doing. I take it that you know nothing of his whereabouts?"

"I'm afraid you're right, sir. He seems to come and go quite unpredictably – it's hard to put your hand on the man." The inspector frowned, and began to pick at his cuffs. "That latest case of his in the paper there," he said, with a gesture towards the newspaper, "and the Hanseatic Bank robbery – what do you make of them?"

"I'm sure you know more than I about these things," I replied. "I haven't seen Holmes since he left for the Continent weeks ago. Evidently he's now back in this country, and too busy to come home yet. I assume he was called away to the Hanseatic Bank immediately after the Birmingham business."

"But what do you make of the way your friend has handled these cases?" insisted Lestrade. His question embarrassed me, for I was obliged to admit to myself that

Holmes did not seem to have been successful in either case. I had wondered if his continental exertions had exhausted him, and I said as much to Lestrade.

"Perhaps," he answered drily. "In any event, there's something wrong. I have spoken with both the officers investigating these two cases, and they are not happy about the part played by your friend Holmes. Neither of them was of the opinion that he had been of any assistance. That's not his job, you may say, to assist the police, but it goes further than that; both men felt that Holmes had actually obstructed their enquiries. I don't say deliberately, of course," the inspector added before I could object to this slur on my friend's honour, "but I do say that he has been obstructing police work. We can't have it, Dr Watson."

"Come now," I answered, "have you not on other occasions thought that he was wasting your time and his own, only to find that he was on the right track after all? I appreciate your anxiety, inspector, but it might be unfounded, you know. Perhaps time will prove him right. It often has before."

Lestrade shook his head. "No, it won't wash. Let me tell you one or two things about the Hanseatic Bank robbery, things that did not appear in the papers, and you'll understand me better. Do you know who called Holmes in? I thought not. It was one of the curious things not mentioned in the newspapers. He called himself in. You may well look surprised, doctor – it's not the usual way of things, even for Mr Holmes. Nevertheless, that is what happened. Let me explain. The day before the ship carrying the diamonds was due to dock, the director of the bank received a telegram from Holmes demanding a meeting. Holmes warned that through his usual network of criminal connections he had learned that a robbery was afoot, and that it was planned to break into the bank's vaults overnight. Together Holmes and the director devised a plan to foil the attempt. The diamond shipment was to be escorted by police to the bank, where it was to be unpacked without delay in the presence of Holmes and the police officers. Once checked, it was to be sorted into separate parcels for the various buyers, and the parcels despatched or collected within a few hours at most. That night, when the gang broke into the vaults, the police would be waiting for them. The risk was slight; for if anything were to go wrong, and the gang somehow succeed in their theft, they would find they had stolen an empty safe-box. Well, you have read in the paper what happened. There was indeed an attempted robbery, not in the night but within a few minutes of the diamonds arriving at the bank. Four or five ruffians tried to force their way into the building; blows were exchanged, and a gun fired. While this fracas was taking place at the entrance, Holmes ordered one of the constables to take the box down to the vault, in case the gang should force its way into the building."

"A wise precaution," I commented.

"I am not so sure of that, as events turned out. The gang was repelled, and off they ran down the street. When the coast was clear, the box was brought back upstairs so that the parcelling out of the diamonds could proceed as planned. The box was empty."

"How on earth could that have happened?" I asked. "Did you not tell me that they checked the diamonds were in the box as soon as it arrived?"

"Quite right, and as far as I can see there is only one explanation: one of the gang must have snatched the diamonds in the confusion."

"Unless an employee of the bank had taken it," I suggested.

"No, that is out of the question. The three bank employees there were all utterly trustworthy men, and not only that – they all emptied their pockets, as did the men from the force, so we know it was no 'inside job'. Even Mr Holmes went along with it, and emptied his pockets too, I'll say that much for him. Now, we all know that Mr Holmes has his own methods, which they aren't regular police methods, and he can take short cuts where we in the Force cannot, and as you know, we sometimes turn a blind eye to his irregular ways and go along with them, because they get results. But when they don't get results, it's a different matter. Then it's harder for us to turn a blind eye. Here, you see, with this robbery at the bank, he has walked in unasked and set up a plan which has allowed diamonds worth almost one million pounds to be stolen from under the noses of the police. It's rank interference, Dr Watson, and we can't have it."

The inspector leaned forward and jabbed his forefinger towards the newspaper I had been reading. "This murder in Birmingham you were reading about – it's the same story there, I'm sorry to say. In comes Mr Holmes, with his short cuts and special methods, and the police investigation goes by the board. Again I say, we'd bear it if he got his man, but he hasn't in this case any more than in the other. I'll tell you about the case, Dr Watson. First of all, we have the discovery of the body of Mr Montague Jarret, a local business man. His housekeeper comes down in the morning and finds Jarret lying dead in the hall, with his skull smashed in. Blood everywhere. Mr Sprague, Jarret's business partner, when he hears about it, asks Holmes to conduct an independent investigation, and Mr Holmes promptly arrives and pronounces it to be a case of burglary, which, given the forced casement, ransacking of the house, and missing items, it didn't need Europe's greatest detective to deduce that. Holmes presents the examining officer with the name of the burglar; a man named Scotty, well known to the police. Off goes Mr Holmes, and off go the police to pick up Scotty. They find him easy enough, the worse for wear after spending spent the night of the murder out drinking with some friends who he can't quite remember exactly who they were. They think they've found their man, but he tells them that from two o'clock in the morning until six o'clock he was in a police cell in Yardley for drunk and disorderly. All well and good; he burgled Jarret's place, they suppose, was surprised by him and killed him, and then got drunk with his friends. But when the police surgeon's report comes in, it says that death took place between four o'clock and five, and certainly no earlier than three o'clock. Impossible, they say, but he won't be budged. So it couldn't have been Scotty, after all, with him being in a police cell at the time; so no suspect, and no Mr Holmes, who by this time, having sent the local force off on a wild-goose chase, has vanished again."

My guest pulled out his watch. "I have taken enough of your time." He stood. "You'll have a word with your friend, I hope. He wouldn't listen to me, even if I could find him, but a friendly word from you might persuade him to take a rest. I'm not here officially, you understand, and we hope it won't become an official matter, but it can't carry on like this, really it can't. He isn't above the law, you know. Goodnight, doctor."

Some days after Inspector Lestrade's visit, when I had

still had no sight of Holmes, a telegram arrived for me at Baker Street.

= ESSENTIAL I HAVE CASE RECORDS FOR LAST THREE YEARS = DELIVER TO BLACK BULL LURKE STREET STEPNEY TOMORROW FRIDAY NOON IN COMPLETE SECRECY = YOU MUST ACT ALONE = I WILL SIGNAL = DO NOT APPROACH = GRAVEST DANGER = HOLMES +

For as long as I had known him, Holmes had kept records and mementoes of all his cases. They were crammed into a large tin box, the size of a small trunk, with rope handles on either end, and my first action on reading his telegram was to drag the box from his room into the parlour. To haul its dead weight across a wooden floor was not too difficult ; but to carry it across London to Stepney would be quite another matter. Even to take it down the stairs would require two pairs of hands, and yet to engage the help of a colleague, however trustworthy he might be, was forbidden by the telegram in clear terms. There was only one answer; I must separate the last three years' cases from the rest, in the hope that they would be compact enough for me alone to carry. The task was no easy one, for the papers were in a state of utter disarray. Some of them gave no year, so that I was obliged to read through them searching for some indication of the date. Many cases, such as the hunting of Captain Falco, were entirely new to me; many more were familiar because I had assisted Holmes in them; the mystery of the moving well of Camber, for instance, and the horrible case of the Four Blind Mice of Dereham Priory, as they became known, a story widely reported in the press at the time. The sheer mass of material was forbidding; but, undeterred, I knelt by the dusty box, as piles of papers grew on the floor around me, and doggedly pored through these relics of Holmes' career, until finally, in the small hours of the night, my task was done and the cases of the last three years were all docketed together. I put them in a stout suitcase and retired gratefully to bed.

The next day, late in the afternoon, I set off in search of the Black Bull in Stepney. As the cab took me eastwards, the busy streets of the city of London gave way to dark, winding lanes where few other carriages were to be seen. No more splendid offices lined the streets; only narrow, hunched rows of sooty houses, or great wharves towering over us where ships debouched cargoes from all parts of the Empire. We twisted and turned and jolted along the cobbled alleys until I had quite lost my bearings, when at a street corner the cab suddenly came to a halt. "The Black Bull!" cried the driver, throwing up the top, and added, grinning down at me, "A very agreeable evening to you!"

The Black Bull stood a storey taller than the neighbouring houses. Squalid and forbidding, its doors and shutters were closed as if its purpose were to repel travellers rather than welcome them. I glanced around me; but for a gang of urchins further up the street throwing stones at a fire-pump, Lurke Street seemed to be deserted. I knocked at the door of the gloomy building, and receiving no reply, I asked myself whether anyone was inside, and whether perhaps I had misread Holmes's telegram and come on the wrong day. But my doubts were unfounded, for at last the door was opened by a large, red-faced man. He looked me up and down.

"Delivery for Mr Sherlock Holmes?" he asked, and put out his hand to take the case.

"That is so," I admitted, "but you will understand that this is a most important package. I must be sure that it is not going into the wrong hands."

The fellow gave a hoarse cackle of appreciation.

"Very good, sir! Quite right, quite right! Cautious is the word. Now, I do believe I can give you that assurance. I'll thank you to look down there in the snug." He stood aside so that I could see past his large frame down a corridor to a cramped public bar where the gas burned low. He turned and called out hoarsely "Mr Holmes!" To my astonishment I saw, in the far side of the room, the familiar figure of my friend rise to his feet. He nodded to me, raised his hand silently, and moved off through a side door.

"You see it's all above-board, Dr Watson," said the man. "Mr Holmes sends his apologies that he must stay in the dark for now. It's a dangerous game he's playing, and he can't risk appearing at the door himself."

I handed the fellow the case, and he bade me good evening and hurriedly closed the door.

My errand accomplished, I was turning to see if my cab had stayed for me, for I had no desire to linger in this shady neighbourhood while night was falling, when I felt a touch on my elbow. It was a policeman. "Excuse me, sir. I believe you are Dr Watson?"

"I am."

He handed me a sheet of paper and shone his torch on it for me.

Kindly do as the constable asks. You will find it a most interesting evening. S.H.

"Would you come with me to that house across the street? Through here, if you will," said the constable, and we entered a house opposite the Black Bull. In the dark we climbed the narrow stairs to the first floor, where he unlocked the door to an empty room. I crossed to the window which gave a view of the inn.

"We must remain in the dark, I'm afraid, sir. We mustn't be seen. Now, you might like to keep your eyes on those first floor windows of the inn."

I looked across to the Black Bull. The place was still dark and lifeless, but after a few minutes a light sprang up in the upstairs window. Somebody was lighting a lamp. The figure bent over it, adjusting the wick, and as the yellow flame flared up it flashed across the hawk-like features of Sherlock Holmes. As he tended the lamp the big man to whom I had spoken earlier entered the room behind him. ("That's the landlord," whispered the policeman.) I watched transfixed as Holmes turned to greet him, and the fellow shambled up to the table where the lamp stood and placed upon it the suitcase I had handed him a few minutes earlier. They exchanged a few words, and the landlord left the room. Holmes opened the case and turned up the light the better to see its contents. He drew out a bundle of papers, and glanced through them; then another, and another; and suddenly he jumped to his feet and clapped his hands together in delight. He then drew up a chair and began to look at the case-records more carefully, reading through the pages one by one with that concentration of attention I knew so well. So absorbed was he as he read that he did not notice that the door behind him was opening. I gave a start on seeing it, but the constable put his hand on my shoulder: "Not a sound, sir," he whispered. "Those are our instructions." Holmes read on, unaware that the door behind him now stood ajar; it was all I could do to restrain myself from banging on the window to warn him of the danger that threatened. The door slowly inched open; I felt the constable's hand clench on my shoulder; across the street Holmes continued to read, hunched over the papers, as behind him the door opened wider and wider, and somebody crept slowly into the room. As the figure entered the circle of lamplight it was revealed as none other than Sherlock Holmes. Suddenly the other Holmes at the table spun round and leapt to his feet, knocking over his chair. His hand went to his coat pocket, but too slowly, for his double, quick as lightning, reached forward with a crop and lashed something from the other's emerging hand. That figure made a grab for the fallen weapon, but again he was too slow, for the other instantly launched himself upon his opponent, sending both crashing into the table. The lamp fell to the floor, where it flared up and rolled wildly to and fro, flinging onto the ceiling gigantic shadows of the struggling figures; then it went out, and all was darkness.

"Follow me!" cried the constable, and we bounded down the stairs and across the street to the Black Bull. We found it still locked; running steps could be heard from within as we hammered on the door. Eventually a policeman opened it to us. "Hello, Jack!" he said, rather out of breath. "Evening, sir! Come inside – two fine birds we have for you, trussed up neat as you like. Your friend Mr Holmes don't mind cutting it fine, does he?"

He led us up the stairs to the front room, where a few candles lit a strange scene. The broken lamp lay on the wooden floor, leaking oil over the scattered case notes, and a chair lay broken beside it. A constable was on his knees retrieving the papers. On the table was the suitcase I had brought, together with many of the case papers, a revolver, and an object a few inches long that I guessed to be the dried skin of a small animal, with some of its hair still attached. By the far wall stood the landlord, flanked by two constables, and not far from him, also between two constables, stood a figure partially resembling Sherlock Holmes. He was of the same height and build as my friend, and of a similarly lean and hollow face. In the manner of his dress too he was the Holmes I knew of old, but the familiar hawk-like nose seemed to have lost its prominence, and the dark hair had become fine and sandy. As I looked him over, his eyes met mine without a trace of warmth or recognition. Before I could address him the door opened again and into the room strode the other Holmes, followed by a police inspector. "Ah, Watson," said the newcomer, "admiring my double? What do you say? Would he pass muster in Madame Tussaud's museum?" He clapped me on the shoulder. "I must thank you, by the bye, for bringing the papers." But for a contusion on the cheek, no doubt a result of the tussle I had just witnessed, he was very evidently in good health and high spirits. "I must thank you, too, inspector, and your men," he said, turning to the policeman. "I should not have relished a confrontation with these fellows without your men to back me."

"You're welcome, Mr Holmes, I'm sure," came the reply. "It's as strange a case as I've ever seen, and I don't expect to see another like it. I'm mighty relieved it's over."

The constable had gathered up the fallen case-notes and put them back in the suit-case. As Holmes went to take the case he paused to pick up the little animal skin that lay beside it on the table. "I'll take this too, if I may," he said, slipping it into his pocket. That done, he seized the case, and we made our farewells and left. Thanks to the kind offices of the inspector a cab awaited us outside, stationed beside the Black Maria that awaited the felons. As we drove back towards Baker Street I begged Holmes to tell me all that had happened in the six or seven weeks since I had last seen him, but to no avail. He insisted that his first requirement was a good supper, and that only then would he satisfy my curiosity. Luckily the resourceful Mrs Hudson was able to provide us with a meal within half an hour of our arrival at Baker Street, and once we both taken our fill, and Mrs Hudson cleared away the plates, we seated ourselves in comfort and Holmes proceeded to enlighten me as to the chain of events that had culminated in the bizarre scene of that evening. It was his custom when working abroad, he reminded me, to keep himself informed of matters of concern at home. To this end he had succeeded in obtaining a delivery of the Times to his Austrian hotel, and had been surprised to read, as he sat in the hotel's lounge, that he was then in London investigating a robbery at the Hanseatic Bank. A few days later, when he was still in Austria, another paper arrived from England, recounting this time his current involvement in a police enquiry into a murder in Birmingham. He determined to find out what was afoot, and decided accordingly to return to England at once incognito, covering his tracks by having false reports spread in the English criminal world to the effect that he was to remain abroad for several weeks longer. Under cover of this pretence, Holmes returned to England and began to search out his double. It soon became apparent to him that the pretender was not acting alone, and that the operation was the work of a well-organised gang. It was, he said with some admiration, a scheme that, despite its risible appearance, presented a grave danger, for not only did the guise of Sherlock Holmes allow the gang unrestricted access to the most promising criminal opportunitites, but the dishonesty and bungling carried out in his name would so damage his reputation that unless the operation were soon stopped his career would be over. He therefore wasted no time in trying to uncover the gang. At first he had little success, for their operation was careful, as well as daring; but eventually they made a mistake. They sent me a telegram, purporting to come from Holmes. The cable gave Holmes a lead that, carefully handled, would bring him to the gang. The situation was one of great delicacy, for if he moved against them prematurely, they would take alarm and go to ground; but he saw in their plan to seize his case records an opportunity to set a trap. He continued to lay low, so that they would press ahead with their plan. As he explained this to me I expressed some disappointment that he had not seen fit to entrust me with the truth of the matter, but I had to confess the justice of his answer, which was that, play-acting not being my forte, a faltering pretence on my part might have aroused their suspicions. He did, however, disclose himself to the police, and together they succeeded in infiltrating the Black Bull at Stepney without raising the suspicions of the gang. And so by my arrival with the papers the trap was sprung, with the results that I myself witnessed. I expressed my surprise that the police had allowed him to confront his double without their support, for his life had hung in the balance. I did not like to think what might have happened had his antagonist been a little quicker in his movements at that moment of reckoning I had witnessed through the window, or had

Holmes's reaction been a little slower. With a laugh he confessed that he had not acted entirely in accord with the plan of attack set by the police. The landlord, as he came downstairs from handing over to his accomplice the suitcase, had been overpowered by three constables, and the plan was that a few minutes later, once the impersonator had made himself at home and become absorbed in the papers, the three men would rush upon him too and overpower him before he had a chance to defend himself. Holmes, however, could not resist silently opening the door and spying upon his mysterious double; and as he watched the man, he could no more resist the impulse to spring upon him and bring the matter to a conclusion. My friend may have had little regard for the ordinary police officer's intelligence, but he had the greatest admiration his fearlessness, and was never prepared to stand by in safety while a brave officer risked his life.

One more thing puzzled me, a trivial enough matter; what, I asked him, was the skin-and-fur thing that I had seen upon the table upstairs in the Black Bull? Holmes brought it from his pocket. "You saw the fellow who played the part of the great Sherlock Holmes," said he. "When you saw him first in the snug of the Black Bull, you mistook him for me, did you not? And yet you saw later that he did not look much like me, after all; he had sandy hair, and a shallow nose. How, then, did you mistake him for me? This is how, Watson," he said, handing me the curious object. "It fell from his face in our little *fracas*." I took the unpleasant thing in my hand and examined it. "It's a kind of half-mask," I exclaimed. "A nose, high and hooked like your own, and above a brow with that widow's peak of black hair."

"Made of gutta percha, putty and horse-hair, I think. Hardly a flattering representation of me, but it served its purpose, and it will serve equally well as a memento of this case," he said, tossing it into the tin box. He leaned back in his chair and put his feet up on the table. "Push the cigar-box my way, there's a good fellow." I did as he asked, first taking a cigar for myself. A grateful silence descended on the room and soon clouds of blue, fragrant smoke rose and billowed over us. "It's a strange and unpleasant thing, Watson, to have a second version of oneself at large. I cannot recommend the experience to you. I do not always see eye to eye with the criminal fraternity, but I think we would agree that one Sherlock Holmes is quite enough."

Acknowledgements

I should like to thank Steve Emecz for all his help. If it had depended on my usual rate of progress, this book would have appeared in the distant future or not at all. It is thanks to Steve's encouragement and energy that it has now seen the light of day.

Also from MX Publishing

 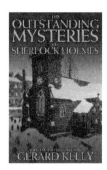 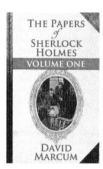

Our bestselling books are our short story collections – of which we have several;

'Lost Stories of Sherlock Holmes' , 'The Outstanding Mysteries of Sherlock Holmes', The Papers of Sherlock Holmes Volume 1 and 2, 'Untold Adventures of Sherlock Holmes' (and the sequel 'Studies in Legacy) and 'Sherlock Holmes in Pursuit', 'The Cotswold Werewolf and Other Stories of Sherlock Holmes' – and many more……

  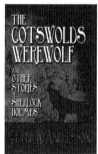

www.mxpublishing.com

Also from MX Publishing

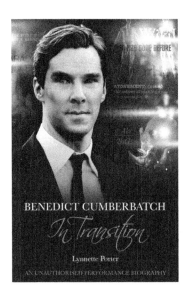

MX Publishing is the world's largest specialist Sherlock Holmes publisher, with over a hundred titles and fifty authors creating the latest in Sherlock Holmes fiction and non-fiction. From traditional short stories and novels to travel guides and quiz books, MX Publishing cater for all Holmes fans. The collection includes leading titles such as *Benedict Cumberbatch In Transition* and *The Norwood Author* the winner of the 2011 Howlett Award (Sherlock Holmes Book of the Year). MX Publishing also has one of the largest communities of Holmes fans on Facebook with regular contributions from dozens of authors.

www.mxpublishing.com

CPSIA information can be obtained
at www.ICGtesting.com
Printed in the USA
LVOW13s1752150518
577262LV00013B/815/P